WHO IS NICK CARTER?

"America's number one espionage agent"
—*Variety*

"The man who inherited the mantle of James Bond" —*Film Daily*

"He stands for counter-intelligence of the highest order"
—*Mike Shane Mystery Magazine*

"The superspy who out-Bonds James Bond, mixing espionage, mayhem, mystery and loving in equal doses" —*Buffalo News*

Nick Carter is the most exciting secret agent in fact or fiction . . . a killer, lover, adventurer, the Intelligence operative who can doublecross, trap or destroy any man—or woman—no matter what gets in his way!

Now . . . follow the espionage adventures of Nick Carter in this taut, tense thriller—HOUR OF THE WOLF.

THE NICK CARTER

AX0238	THE DEVIL'S COCKPIT		AS0921	THE SEA TRAP
AX0277	THE BRIGHT BLUE DEATH		AS0923	DOUBLE IDENTITY
			AS0928	THE AMAZON
AX0288	WEB OF SPIES		AS0938	CARNIVAL FOR KILLING
AX0289	SPY CASTLE			
AX0295	OPERATION MOON ROCKET		AS0940	THE CHINESE PAYMASTER
AX0310	THE TERRIBLE ONES		AS0941	THE DOOMSDAY FORMULA
AX0311	DRAGON FLAME			
AX0312	HANOI		AN1001	THE CAIRO MAFIA
AX0313	OPERATION STARVATION		AN1016	THE INCA DEATH SQUAD
AX0423	THE RED RAYS		AN1033	THE OMEGA TERROR
AX0424	PEKING/THE TULIP AFFAIR		AN1088	ICE BOMB ZERO
			AN1089	THE RED GUARD
AX0455	BERLIN		AN1090	JEWEL OF DOOM
AX0509	OPERATION CHE GUEVARA		AN1091	MOSCOW
			AN1093	THE MIND KILLERS
AX0559	OPERATION SNAKE		AN1094	THE WEAPON OF NIGHT
AX0560	THE CASBAH KILLERS			
AX0583	THE ARAB PLAGUE		AN1095	ISTANBUL
AX0584	THE RED REBELLION		AN1097	RHODESIA
AX0622	RUN, SPY, RUN		AN1098	MARK OF COSA NOSTRA
AX0623	SAFARI FOR SPIES			
AX0625	SAIGON		AN1099	MACAO
AX0628	AMSTERDAM		AN1100	THE 13TH SPY
AX0632	MISSION TO VENICE		AN1101	FRAULEIN SPY
AX0634	A KOREAN TIGER		AN1102	THE GOLDEN SERPENT
AX0636	THE MIND POISONERS			
AX0638	THE CHINA DOLL		AN1103	THE LIVING DEATH
AX0639	CHECKMATE IN RIO		AN1109	BUTCHER OF BELGRADE
AX0686	CAMBODIA			
AS0703	THE DEATH STRAIN		AN1127	THE LIQUIDATOR

KILLMASTER SERIES

AN1132	EYES OF THE TIGER
AN1133	THE DEVIL'S DOZEN
AN1146	THE CODE
AN1160	OUR AGENT IN ROME IS MISSING . . .
AN1166	THE SPANISH CONNECTION
AN1177	DANGER KEY
AN1178	THE DEATH'S HEAD CONSPIRACY
AN1218	ASSIGNMENT: ISRAEL
AN1227	ICE TRAP TERROR
AN1228	HOOD OF DEATH
AN1244	THE COBRA KILL
AN1263	VATICAN VENDETTA
AN1264	THE DEFECTOR
AN1270	SIGN OF THE COBRA
AN1271	A BULLET FOR FIDEL
AQ1297	THE MAN WHO SOLD DEATH
AQ1298	STRIKE FORCE TERROR
AQ1329	CODE NAME: WEREWOLF
AQ1331	NIGHT OF THE AVENGER
AQ1332	THE N3 CONSPIRACY
AQ1333	THE BEIRUT INCIDENT
AQ1354	DEATH OF THE FALCON
AQ1356	THE AZTEC AVENGER
AQ1370	TIME CLOCK OF DEATH
AQ1387	HOUR OF THE WOLF
AQ1388	THE PEKING DOSSIER
AQ1393	SEVEN AGAINST GREECE
AQ1400	THE JERUSALEM FILE
AQ1401	THE BLACK DEATH
AQ1414	TARGET DOOMSDAY ISLAND
AQ1415	THE FILTHY FIVE
AY1424	DR. DEATH
AQ1439	COUNTERFEIT AGENT
AQ1440	TEMPLE OF FEAR
AQ1448	14 SECONDS TO HELL
AQ1449	SIX BLOODY SUMMER DAYS
AQ1454	ASSASSIN: CODE NAME VULTURE
AQ1455	MASSACRE IN MILAN
AQ1456	ASSASSINATION BRIGADE
AQ1477	AGENT COUNTER-AGENT
AQ1460	THE Z DOCUMENT
AQ1474	THE HUMAN TIME BOMB
AQ1479	THE KATMANDU CONTRACT
AQ1486	THE ULTIMATE CODE
AQ1490	ASSAULT ON ENGLAND
AQ1493	THE EXECUTIONERS
AQ1501	THE JUDAS SPY
AQ1502	THE KREMLIN FILE

NICK CARTER

A Killmaster Spy Chiller.

THE KREMLIN FILE

AWARD
BOOKS
NEW YORK

PRINTING HISTORY

First Award Printing.........September 1973
Second Printing ....December 1975

AWARD BOOKS are published by
Universal-Award House, Inc., a subsidiary of
Universal Publishing and Distributing Corporation
235 East Forty-fifth Street, New York, N.Y. 10017.

Manufactured in the United States of America

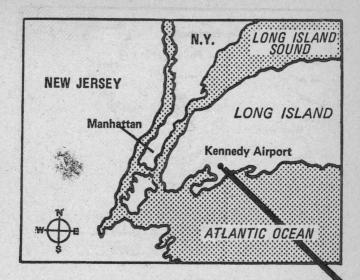

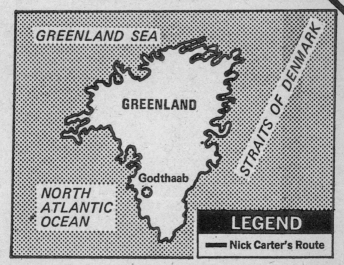

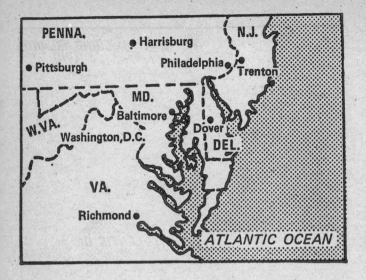

ONE

It's impossible now to skyjack a plane from the United States. You know it can't be done, and I know it—and so does every idiot who gets hold of a Saturday Night Special or an army surplus grenade.

So why was the stewardess on Flight 709, bound for Grand LaClare Island, being so cozy with the black haired, dark faced passenger at the head of the aisle? She was passing him a gun.

A tidy little snubnosed job all warmed up from lying under her uniform, between the fantastic breasts I'd just been admiring so much. Everybody seemed to be asleep, and at first I thought the man was feeling her up and she was being an obliging hostess. "I'm Reddy. Fly me." When she unzipped her fitted jacket, I figured I was in for some entertaining voyeurism. Until she took out the shiny little piece of metal that caught a glint of light and winked at me.

She laid it in his palm, turned her back and went through the door to the front cabin.

The man stood close to the door between the two heads, looking back along the plane, holding the gun in plain sight. My Luger hung in its shoulder clip, but I knew any movement I made to reach it would

9

draw attention. The stiletto in the chamois sheath on my right forearm would snap down to my hand invisibly enough, but throwing it was something else. The man would see it, and he'd be able to get off a shot before I could hit him.

While I was still trying to decide what action might be possible, the decision was taken out of my hands. The noise of a shot in the cockpit woke everybody. I heard grunts and gasps and people started up in the seats, then the man's voice overrode the sounds.

"Remain calm. The plane is being diverted. In Havana you will all be released unhurt so do not be afraid."

He had an accent, Spanish. Beside me Tara Sawyer vented a low groan, and beyond her Randolph Fleming sucked in his breath.

"Be quiet. Sit still." I whispered it without moving my lips and my voice didn't carry beyond our seats.

The girl whispered back. Try to stop a woman talking. "Cuba? With the antihijack treaty?"

It wasn't the time to explain that the only people who could count on refuge in Cuba would be agents for Castro or his big Red friend across the waters. But if she'd shut up and think, she could figure it out herself. She was smart enough.

I watched the man's black eyes play over the passengers, working back along the plane. They paused for a split second on us, then lifted to see what the reaction was behind us.

I turned slowly, as if to speak to the girl at my side, and with my twisted shoulder as cover slid my hand under my lapel for the Luger. The man did not drop his glance. No passenger would be expected to be armed. I eased the gun into my lap and switched it to my left hand. I was in the aisle seat on the right of the plane and I could get a clear shot from the level of the arm rest. I squeezed the trigger.

The little weapon spun out of his hand and I fired a second time. The front of his white shirt bloomed red. He slammed back against the door and hung as if he were nailed there, his mouth dropping open for a scream that did not come. Then his knees gave and he crumpled. The door jarred against him but his body kept it from opening. I had moved as soon as I fired. Behind me a woman yelled. Hysteria was building all around.

I yanked on a dead foot, pulled the body away and the door swung toward me. The stewardess stood there, gun in hand. The bullet whispered between my raised arm and my side, cut through my coat, sped on and a scream from the rear of the plane told me someone had been hit. Then I had the girl's wrist, forcing it down and twisting until her fingers opened and her gun fell.

She fought me, clawing at my face with long, sharp nails and I dropped the Luger to use the side of my hand in a karate chop against her neck. She went out like a light. I flung her behind me on top of the corpse and scooped up all three guns, dropped two in my pocket and kept hold of the Luger. I didn't want her waking up and tossing lead at my back.

I didn't know what I'd find in the cockpit. The plane was tipping, banking, changing course, then falling off on one wing out of control, sliding toward the dark sea. Either way it threw me off balance and I ducked through the door, bracing against the jamb.

The pilot was sprawled half out of his seat across the wheel, locking it for a dive. Blood leaked from a hole in his back. The navigator was hunched over the wounded man. The copilot was fighting the ship back to straight and level flight. I didn't interrupt them. The navigator got the pilot off his wheel and whipped out a handkerchief to mop at the blood. It was like trying to stop Niagara Falls. The copilot got the plane straight and switched it on automatic pilot. He turned to help the navigator, saw me, the gun in my hand, and froze. I knew he thought I was another skyjacker.

"Relax," I told him and shoved the Luger back in its clip. "Take a deep breath and set her back on course for Grand LaClare. They lost the game."

The copilot stared past me at the rubbish on the floor. The navigator whirled, one hand holding the pilot against the seat, and gaped at me white-faced.

"Who the hell are you?"

"Johnny on the Spot, call it." I nodded toward the pilot. "Is he dead?"

The man shook his head, then dropped his eyes to the aisle. The copilot spoke in a daze.

"She shot Howie . . . the *stewardess!*" The way he said it, he might have been talking about the First Lady. Then his mind clicked into gear. "You . . . Hey . . . What are you doing with a gun?"

I grinned at him. "Aren't you glad I have it? You'd better call Kennedy and report. You can ask

them if Nick Carter has permission to carry arms
aboard. Tell them to query Timothy Whiteside. He's
president of this airline, in case you've forgotten."

The pair looked at each other, then the copilot
dropped back to his seat, obviously reluctant to take
his eyes off me, and radioed the airport. It was a
while before the answer graveled through the mike.
Probably Whiteside had to be routed out of bed. But
when it came, in a direct quote relayed from his office, his clearance of me was earthy and explosive,
due I suspected to the shock of hearing how one of
his proud flights had been abused.

By that time the other two stewardesses had come
running, poked their heads into the cabin, sized up
the situation and ducked back, one using the PA to
make reassuring noises and the other moving along
the aisle trying to quiet the frightened, panicky passengers.

I touched the pilot's wrist and found the pulse ragged and weakening. I told the navigator, "I'll give
you a hand, take him out to those empty seats at the
tail."

He was still wary of me, but he needed my help.
We untangled the pilot and carried him awkwardly
over the inert figures blocking the passage and on to
where a blonde in uniform had the wit to pull the
arms out from between the seats in a row of three.
The "couch" we had wasn't long enough and the pilot's legs hung over when we laid him on his stomach, but I didn't think he knew or would care for
very long.

A hostess brought a first aid kit and Tara Sawyer came up beside her, saying quietly, "Let me. I know how and you have enough to do."

The navigator and I left the girls to work it out and went to move the unconscious stewardess to an empty seat behind the pilot. I felt over her with my hands in case the little walking arsenal had other guns, but she was clean. I borrowed bandage enough from the kit to tie her hands behind her back and wrap her ankles together—just in case she came to and made a try for the target with her bare claws. We stashed the dead hijacker out of sight in a head and returned to the cockpit.

The copilot still looked pale and worried, asking how the pilot was doing, and looked worse when I said not good.

"Damn them." It was half a cry. "How could they get aboard with those guns? How did you?"

"Special privilege for me. The girl slipped two into her bra. Cute. Your crews aren't subject to search, are they?"

Both men made growling noises over that loophole in security. I wondered how deeply the copilot was jolted. There was still a long flight ahead.

I said, "You able to fly her clear to Port of Spain or do you want me to spell you?"

His eyebrows climbed up his forehead. "You mean you have a license to fly these babies?"

I took out my wallet and showed him the paper. He shook his head.

"Thanks for the offer but I can take her in."

"Sing out if you change your mind. I'll be around. Close."

That brought a laugh I hoped would relieve his tension and I left. One stewardess was serving drinks free to tempt the passengers out of their obvious hysteria and the other was administering oxygen to an elderly man who appeared to have had a heart attack. Tara Sawyer still worked over the pilot, cool and efficient. The more I saw of her, the better I felt about her. Not many women would be this calm under the circumstances. She looked at me as I stopped beside her and said almost under her breath, "He isn't going to make it, Nick."

"I know. I can see it."

I sighed and turned my attention to the stewardess with the guns. I saw her stir, open her eyes and try to lift a hand to the red welt on her neck. She looked down quickly, trying to see behind her but the pain of the movement brought her jerking upright.

"Oh. . ." It was a gasp. "My neck . . . . It hurts." She raised her eyes to mine.

"It isn't broken," I told her. "And you're a lousy shot."

Her mouth turned down and she moaned, closing her eyes. I didn't want her passing out again so I called another stewardess over to help. I told her to bring a glass with half water, half whiskey, and to see that her buddy drank it. She followed orders well, bending over the girl in the seat, holding her chin and tipping the head up, pouring into the mouth when it winced with pain. The girl swallowed, choked, gagged, breathed deeply and the stewardess poured again on top of the indrawn air. Part of that mouthful spilled down the uniform.

I asked, "Did you ever see her before this flight?"

The stewardess straightened, a tall beauty whose gray eyes smoked and whose voice, now that she was through nursemaiding her passengers, was clipped, tight with anger.

"Not until she showed up in the ready room. Our regular on this run, Edith, called in just before flight time, and said she was sick but was sending a friend to fill in. Some friend."

"Does that happen often?"

"First time I know of. Normally we have regular standbys but tonight none of those girls came in."

I frowned. "Didn't that strike anybody as more than coincidence?"

The stew's lips curled in a sardonic grimace of aggrieved helplessness. "Mister, in the airline business anything can happen and mostly does, always at the last minute. We quizzed her and she knew the job so we brought her along. What kind of a cop are you anyway?"

"A lucky one, tonight. Do you think you could find a blanket to cover the pilot? People seem to be staring."

She threw another bitter look at the redhead and sashayed away, her pretty rump twitching in indignation. The ringer in the seat ignored her, watching me the way a wounded bird on the ground watches a hungry cat. I stepped across her feet and sat down beside her. Women talk to me better if I don't scare them so I looked sympathetic, even apologetic.

"Your looks aren't going to last out the prison term, honey. It's a murder charge for killing the captain plus whatever they throw at you for the skyjack attempt. But if you level with me and I like your answers, I can get you a break. What's your name?"

Hope and pleading came through the husky voice. "Mary Austin."

"And your boyfriend's?"

"Juan. . . Cardoza. . . Where is he?"

I hit her with it. "Dead."

I wanted her reaction. It could tell me whether she knew what she was mixed up in or was a dupe only. Her face crumpled as though I had cut into her heart. Her eyes flooded with tears and pain. She was genuinely grieved.

I asked her gently, "Tell me about Juan, Mary, who he was."

The voice had lost its life. "Just a Cuban exile. He was broke and he had to go back. He said he was a relative of Castro's so they wouldn't do anything to him."

Juan sounded more like a member of the secret police, I thought. That was the trouble with letting in exiles—you couldn't be sure who was legitimate and who was working for an enemy.

I said, "How long did you know him?"

"Six months." It was a child crying over a broken doll. "I met him when I was working for Eastern, on a run from Miami. Then two weeks ago he asked me to quit. He needed my help. He was inheriting a lot of money in Cuba and when he got it we could get married. Now . . . you killed him."

"Wrong, Mary, you killed him when you passed him that gun and shot the pilot."

She was crying aloud. People were staring with puzzled faces, some angry, some still frightened.

"I shot . . . it was accident . . . the navigator jumped . . . he startled me . . . I just squeezed. . . . I didn't mean . . . I never meant. . . . I only wanted them to turn. . . ."

I stood up, pulled out the arm rests and hefted her onto the seats. I left her alone to cry it out. Later, maybe, I could sell Hawk on getting the charges softened somewhat for her. Obviously she had never heard of the first rule of weaponry—never pull a gun unless you mean to fire it. The second rule ought to be that children shouldn't play with guns.

TWO

My boss, David Hawk, has a way with him. When he calls me N3, my official code name as a senior Killmaster, I know he is going to ram a really tough job down my throat.

Ordinarily, when we are alone, he calls me Nick. But when he coughs and says "N3" I want to double my life insurance, though I haven't any since no company is idiot enough to issue me a policy.

I had come to his office to make my report. AXE has the lousiest headquarters of any of the government investigating agencies. The CIA and FBI boys wouldn't be caught dead in a place like this, and the Secret Service people are even harder to please. Because they guard the President, they consider themselves a cut above the rest of us.

I had just gotten back from Greenland, where the Russian fishing fleet had been quietly building a submarine base in territory where they had no business to be. The base had mysteriously blown up, a nice accomplishment on my part, considering that none of the Ruskies had dreamed I was within five thousand miles.

I was tired. I was looking forward to a couple of weeks of innocent ice fishing in northern Michigan while my blood was still conditioned to cold weather. Instead Hawk shoved a newspaper across his desk, caughed, and said, "N3, what does that mean to you?"

I could have answered before I read the headline —trouble. The screamer didn't disappoint me.

GENERAL ABLE HAMMOND KILLED IN AIR CRASH

I don't suppose one out of a hundred thousand Americans could identify Hammond. You had to have taken a Caribbean cruise that put in at Grand LaClare Island. The general had been dictator there.

The island had a long and troubled history. First settled by the Spanish, it had fallen into French hands and then been taken over by the British. The population was 90 percent black, descendants of the slaves brought from Africa to work the sugar plantations and the rich forests. In an election ten years ago, the islanders had voted to break with the British Empire and establish their own republic, with Dr. Randolph Fleming as the first president.

Fleming was the most competent and by far the most popular man on Grand LaClare. He reformed the government and became a true father of his country. Then he was overthrown. He hadn't kowtowed to the military, and they had rebelled. General Hammond had led the coup, and Fleming had run for his life, seeking asylum in the States. Hammond took over. As the military always does he rode roughshod over the people and bled the country dry. Now Hammond was dead, whether by design or accident did not matter. He left a vacuum. Anybody who had shown traces of leadership had been jailed or had disappeared, and I was afraid I knew who our diplomats had in mind to lend a helping hand over there.

Hawk growled out a warning. "We have information that the Russians are preparing to move in missles. Everything is being done very quietly, you understand, and that's why we have to move undercover too.

"To divert us, Cuba's been making noises about 'helping out' its needy neighbor on Grand LaClare. But we know the Soviets are pulling the strings and the purpose of the 'aid' is to install Red missiles. So this operation is going into the Kremlin file."

David Hawk drummed on the edge of his desk with blunt fingertips and told me serenely, "It's a one-man operation, N3. Our government doesn't want another Cuban-invasion deal. It's your job to get Randolph Fleming back to Grand LaClare as quickly as possible."

I didn't think their army would sit still for that and said so.

"It's up to you, N3, to see they do. You'll have to anchor Fleming solidly in the presidential palace. And you'll have to do it without letting anyone know this country had a hand in the matter."

I let my sarcasm show. "I'm used to being shot at, knifed, poisoned, threatened in every way you can name, but I never discovered a way to make myself invisible. Will you please tell me how?"

There are a lot of things I am good at, but ruffling

David Hawk is not one of them. He is unflappable. He didn't even smile.

"It's been taken care of already. Fortunately, Fleming and Tom Sawyer are old, close friends."

"I like Huck Finn better, but how does Mark Twain's book help me?"

Hawk doesn't appreciate flippancy and he told me sourly, "Thomas Sawyer. You may have heard he is president of the Sawyer hotel chain, now the largest such organization in the world.

"Three years ago Sawyer made a deal with General Hammond. He was given a two-square-mile plot of land along the beach on which he built a luxury hotel featuring a casino to cater to the free-spending tourists. It's been a bonanza for both Sawyer and the General.

"Obviously, the Sawyer interests are very much opposed to a communist government coming into power. They would nationalize Sawyer's holdings as one of their acts. So you can see why Tom Sawyer is willing, I'd say anxious, to foot the bill for our operation in return for Fleming's promise that Sawyer's business will be safe. Fleming has already given his word."

I nodded. To use a hackneyed phrase, politics makes strange bedfellows. Fleming, the patriot, with Sawyer, the ruthless wheeler-dealer. And I was going to have to make the best and most of it. I left the dingy office thinking ill of the world.

The Sawyer New Yorker was typical of chain-operated hotels: a small lobby surrounded by expensive shops. There was one difference in this place, a private elevator that serviced the penthouse only.

The car fired up thirty stories to a richly carpeted hall where an elegant blonde waited for me. The corridor was a gallery of high-priced art but I hardly noticed the pictures. The blonde was better to look at than any of them. She smiled and offered a slim hand that collapsed at the knuckles, an erotic surprise that got to me.

"Mr. Carter?"

"That's me."

"I am Tara Sawyer," she said. "Father is on the telephone, as usual, and I'm to take you in."

She tucked my hand under her arm, matching me stride for stride down the hall and through a door at the end. The room beyond could have held a convention with ease. At the far end a plate glass wall revealed a terrace forested with tubbed evergreens. There was no desk in sight, no files, only luxurious carpeting with islands of chairs and lounges. And a bar. The other half lived well. The girl homed in on the bar and let go of me finally.

"What would you like to wait with, Mr. Carter?"

"Brandy, please."

She sloshed an inch into a snifter for me and built herself a scotch and soda while I warmed the glass in both hands. Then we carried the drinks to the glass wall and looked across the terrace, down on the snow in the park far below.

"It's a shame," she said in irritation. "All that open space and no one dares use it after dark. A disgrace."

I thought of but did not mention a lot of places, open and closed, that were not safe for some people even in daylight. This room might have been one of them for Tara Sawyer if the parental presence was not so imminent. She was very tempting, a lot of woman under the slim, tailored pantsuit that clung to her firm thighs and hung softly over her breasts. I raised my snifter in a silent toast, letting her see my admiration. Then the door behind us opened and closed and that was that.

Thomas Sawyer in the flesh was a letdown. I had assumed the tycoon would reflect his overwhelming success, and expected to see an outsized man charged full of electric energy. Instead, he was about five foot four, half a head shorter than his daughter, birdlike in his quick movements, robust only in the surprisingly deep voice. He stopped a few feet from us, looked me up and down, appraising, the way he would when buying a car, or a man.

"Mr. Carter?" He wasn't sure.

I dipped my head.

"You are not at all what I expected."

He wasn't complaining and I knew what he meant. Most people picture an agent as a cross between Bogart and Sir John Ogilvie Rennie, the poor joker the British M.I.6 Department called "C," the man whose cover was blown by the German magazine *Stern*. He was retired on a pension but he was a natural for Central Casting as a spy. I just don't look the part.

"I'd really enjoy sitting down with you and having a long talk," the hotel magnate went on. "But that will have to wait. You and Tara have a plane to catch and time is getting short. You are to leave Kennedy at twelve thirty-five."

David Hawk throws me a lot of curves but hardly ever any like this. The curves on the blonde girl were just dandy and she was coming along. Just for the ride? Things were looking better by the minute.

I touched her elbow. "If you're packed, we'd better shove. My bags are downstairs but I have to see a man at the airport before we take off."

She walked into another room and Sawyer took me to the corridor door. She was back in a moment in a mink hat, mink coat open over a soft blue dress. She brought only one small suitcase, a restraint I approved, and tossed it to me from three feet away. Maybe to see if I could catch it without a warning. I did. She bent to kiss her father, patted him on the head and we left.

In the limousine, a lovely thing long enough to make a Mafia cruiser look like a Toyota, she closed the glass between us and the chauffeur and turned unexpectedly businesslike, saying earnestly, "Now we have time for me to cue you in on some items. Dr. Fleming must not know who you really are or why you're going to the island. He is to think you are only in Dad's employ as a security officer for the hotel. He has a strange pride, an innocence if you will, and if he learned anyone other than his own people were putting him back in the palace, he would refuse to take the presidency."

"Oh?" I watched her face. "Isn't he aware your father bought the army?"

The corner of her mouth tucked in at the word but

she didn't evade the issue. "He has no idea and he must not find out. He thinks the army feels there is no one else capable of managing the country now. But my father doesn't trust the military to keep its word and you'll have to stay awake."

I got the idea then. Papa was sending Baby along to watch me and to see the assignment through. It wasn't just the LaClare army he didn't trust. He didn't trust AXE or me and he was willing to put his luscious daughter out as bait to make sure all went A-O.K. Well, that was one bribe I'd be happy to accept.

I said, "In that case, the three of us shouldn't appear to be together. Thomas Sawyer's daughter would not travel with a flunky as a companion and neither would Dr. Fleming. I'll leave it to you to handle the matter."

I had her drop me off and caught a cab so we could arrive at Kennedy separately. Also, I had good reason for not wanting her along on my next errand. I hunted up the airline office in Manhattan, showed my ID to the president, and had him check by phone with AXE's Washington headquarters. I had to board the plane with my weapons and I didn't want any disturbance at the gate to call attention to me.

The man was impressed with Hawk's answer and called his manager at the airport so that when I arrived, I was personally escorted onto the plane.

Tara Sawyer was already there, talking with a scholarly, handsome blue-black man in the window seat of a three place row. I assumed that was Dr. Randolph Fleming, Thomas Sawyer's expensive new president of Grand LaClare Island. I glanced at him as I sat down beside the girl and saw compelling level brown eyes and an aura of leadership and integrity. He gave me one brief look then dismissed me as a simple necessity. I read his mind. Once he reached the island, he would feel secure; but until he was in the presidential palace, he was an easy target.

I wondered why a dollop of Sawyer's millions had not been used to get us a private plane and decided on the pride Tara had talked about—probably, Fleming wouldn't accept that precaution; it smacked of a coward's return.

Fleming's voice was soft, his words measured and he talked to Tara Sawyer with a restrained solemnity. They could pass for strangers making casual conversation. We got into the air and the stewardesses brought blankets and pillows. Soon most of the lights winked out and the ship settled down to sleep.

Except for Tara and me. Being so close together for a long night created one hell of a temptation to both of us, but there wasn't a thing we could do about it except sit and sweat it out. Fortunately it kept us awake.

I didn't get an introduction to Fleming until after the skyjacking incident was under control. Then he grudgingly admitted it was a fortunate coincidence that the Sawyer Grand LaClare's new security officer happened to be taking this flight. He hoped I would like his island and his people.

Then, as an example to the still jittery passengers, he tipped his seat back and went peacefully to sleep.

THREE

The Grand LaClare airport wasn't as big as O'Hare but it was as crowded as if the Chicago field had dumped all its passengers there. It was so modern I thought General Hammond might have gotten the financing for it out of his Sawyer casino-hotel deal. The native mob was in multi-colored costumes, kept back from the plane by a cordon of soldiers in dress shorts and short-sleeved shirts. They looked like Boy Scouts except for the side arms. A solid rank of them surrounded the plane and stood around a waiting group of limousines.

A stewardess announced that all of us must keep our seats until Dr. Fleming had left the field. The ladder was run out and the door opened. I had seen the huge crowd from the inside; now I heard a roar rise to a crescendo as the new president of the island stepped into sight. He looked every inch the head of state.

Beside me Tara Sawyer whispered, "Look at that man. I wish we were on the ground to see him come down."

"You won't get trampled to mush up here. Be thankful," I told her.

Watching from the window, we saw Fleming again as he reached the bottom of the steps and lifted a paternal hand to the islanders. A thickset man in a bright uniform snapped to sharp attention, threw a crisp salute, then stepped close to shake the Doctor's hand. Fleming smiled.

"Colonel Carib Jerome," Myra said. "Chief of Staff of the army. The man who engineered Fleming's return."

That was my contact. I looked him over closely. The black face was not Negroid. His eyes slanted Oriental fashion, the cheekbones were high, the ripe olive skin marked him as a descendant of the Brazilian Indians who had invaded Grand LaClare in prehistoric times. He could pass for a taller, darker Vietnamese. Jerome put his lips near Fleming's ear to be heard above the happy hysteria. From his watchfulness I judged he was warning of possible danger. He took Fleming's arm to turn him directly toward the waiting cars.

Fleming smiled, shook off the hand and went confidently into the crowd. He walked beside the cordon of soldiers, reaching for the hands enthusiastically stretched through it. The pandemonium didn't diminish even after he entered the long black car with the official flags on its fenders; some of the crowd surged after the motorcycles that crawled to the road.

We had to wait further inside the plane while military police boarded to take off the stewardess who'd tried to hijack the craft. She met my eyes as they walked her past, frightened and pleading. I smiled and nodded. Maybe I could get her a lighter sentence; she was more victim than villain. Surrounded by soldiers, the crowd took her for a VIP and screamed until she was out of sight in the terminal. Obviously, the hijacking had not been announced to the public.

After that the passengers were allowed to deplane. The crowd still cheered. We had ridden with the illustrious Dr. Fleming. Tara laughed and waved and they focused on her. Nobody paid attention to me. I like it that way. It's a big asset to an agent not to be noticed. We were herded into the comparative quiet of the Customs shed and lined up along the low baggage bench. After a short wait, the luggage began coming along on a moving belt behind the inspectors. I pointed out Tara's and mine; they were set before us and we were asked to open them.

The examination was unexpectedly thorough. In the Caribbean the Customs people are usually cavalier. They're dealing with tourists they don't want to offend. What really surprised me here was the frisk. The man felt my holster, opened my jacket and grunted at the Luger.

"Explain, please." The voice said I was not a rich visitor to be pampered.

I said I was the new chief security officer for Sawyer's hotel. He was not impressed, snapped his fingers for two policemen trying to be inconspicuous in the background, and ordered me taken to the station for questioning. I was relieved of the gun. Tara wanted to go to bat right there. I stepped on her toe. No point in her being entangled in bureaucratic red tape. I said I'd meet her later at the hotel and went with the police to a van behind the building. They let me bring my bag. David Hawk would have the spitting meemies. He had an agent's contempt for the bumbles of regular cops.

It was a ten mile ride to the capital city, and slow. The roadside was still jammed and ahead of us Fleming's cortege was making the most of political hay, going five miles an hour to give the population a good look at their man. We crawled behind the rear escort. The men taking me in were like cops anywhere, bored with the duty. Jerome had proclaimed a legal holiday and a fiesta for the night. It meant only extra hours of work to this pair.

People were still three and four deep as we passed the Sawyer hotel. The vast lawn was peppered with curious tourists, dwarfed in front of the mammoth, pale pink monument to fun. The architecture was sterile, designed to awe the guests and not distract them from the main objective of passing their dollars across the gaming tables under the illusion they were being entertained. The building sprawled across the waterfront between the harbor and the wide boulevard at the edge of a solid business district. Beyond it I saw three cruise ships at anchor; with the swarm from those boats plus the plane influx the casino must be jumping.

The police station was tucked away where it wouldn't jar the sensibilities of visitors. It was as new as the airport. Sawyer had paid handsomely for his land and rights. There was a small plaque on the waiting room wall giving credit to his generosity. I was taken in through a rear door. The phony stewardess who had shot the pilot sat on a wooden bench, handcuffed to it, weeping slow tears, left in limbo to build horrid fantasies of what would happen to her. I sat down beside her, massaged her taut neck, told her to stick to the truth, and said again I'd intercede. She was too cute to waste away in a women's prison. She gave me a wan smile, put her head on my shoulder and got it wet. A matron came and took her away. They didn't want her depression eased.

I was left alone for an hour. The worry treatment. I worried. I couldn't blow my cover and it would be embarrassing to ask Sawyer to pull rank for me so soon. I had to stay put and play the silly game, see where it led and go from there.

Two men finally dropped the shoe, coming through a door labeled administration. One was the cop who had driven the van, the other wore civilian whites.

"Sorry to keep you waiting," white-suit said. He didn't sound sorry, but veddy veddy British. It startles most Americans to hear a black islander clip his words like an Oxford don. "Why did you wear a gun?"

I didn't tell him. I said, "That's the way I carry it."

He didn't like it. "Only our island authorities are permitted to bear arms, Mr. Carter. You have violated. . . ."

"As chief of security for the biggest hotel here, don't I qualify as authority?"

"Only within that property. As I was about to say, you have violated our constitution, which is grounds for your expulsion from this country."

I grinned at him, picturing David Hawk's apoplexy if I phoned to say I was being deported. It was time to apply acupuncture to authority's nerve chain of command.

I said thoughtfully, "I'd better call Tom Sawyer and tell him. He won't be happy."

That stung. A finger ran around inside his shirt collar as though it were a tightening noose.

"You . . . ah . . . have a personal acquaintance with Mr. Sawyer?"

"We're half brothers. He's the elder."

"Uh . . . I'll make further inquiries of my . . . uh, superiors." He looked a trifle peaked and turned to the cop. "Howard, hold him in the detention pen while I see what. . . ." He let the sentence trail off, he was in such a hurry to be out the door.

Neither of them could work in my bureaucracy or on my police force. The gun had thrown them in such a tizzy they hadn't thought to look further. Nobody had found the thin stiletto against my forearm. I didn't want to make any more waves until I had to. News of my part in the hijack attempt apparently had not filtered down to this level, but a higher official ought to know and react to that. I went with meekly Howard through the booking office, down a corridor between cells to a tank at the end.

The place was oblong-shaped with facing benches against two walls. A fat man I took to be an American salesman slumped on one, drunk, one eye turning purple, cowering at the back corner as far as he could get from the other occupant. That was a Negro, big, mean, ugly, stretched out on the other slab. He lay there until Howard went away and the corridor gate clanged after him, then he unfolded, stood up grinning, and tried to walk a circle around me. I turned with him.

"Stay still," he said.

He tried to walk behind me again but I kept facing him. Without warning he shot a fist at my middle. I took the wrist and flipped him over my head to the floor on his back. He looked pleased, as if that was what he wanted, and came up to a crouch ready to lunge. When he saw the stiletto waiting to take his gut out, he backed off, shrugged, and sat down. I got the idea he wasn't really interested in trouble, that he had a job, was paid to put prisoners in the proper frame of mind to ante up anything the jailer asked or confess whatever the cops wanted. I had thought of catching a nap while I waited, but decided against it now and sat on the other end of the bench from the drunk, keeping an eye on the big black man.

He didn't move again for the next half hour. Then a cop I hadn't seen before came, opened the door and waved me out. The drunk tried to rush to the opening but the Negro caught him and knocked him down. I used the edge of my hand against the thick neck and dropped him. I stared at the cop until his eyes fell.

"Put him somewhere else," I said. "Or I'll talk to our consul." In any event I meant to get word to Fleming that this pigsty needed hosing down.

From the cop's expression he thought so too. It was in his favor that he dragged the unconscious man out to the corridor, left him there, locked the grille and steered me back to the booking office.

Tara Sawyer was there, holding my Luger. For an improbable moment I thought she was helping me break out. She was indignant enough. But three policemen stood behind her, nervously, and the man who had questioned me was in a sweat.

"Your arrest was a mistake, Mr. Carter. I apologize for uh . . . the misunderstanding." He gave me my suitcase.

He bobbled for apples while Tara passed me the gun. I holstered it and we went out through the door he held open. One thing the jail had going for it—it was cooler than the street. Even in 74-degree February the pavement and the buildings bounced heat at us. I raised an eyebrow at the girl. She was still huffy.

"How ridiculous. I went straight to Dr. Fleming; his first official act was to order your release and give you permission to carry that gun anywhere you want on Grand LaClare Island. And Nick, today Fleming's addressing Parliament in special session at Government House. He gave us tickets to the visitors' gallery, he wants you to hear him. One-thirty. We have time for drinks and lunch."

I leered at her. "Is that all?"

She hugged my arm. "Before the speech, yes. With you, I don't want to be rushed, and I'm too famished to pass up food."

There wasn't a chance of getting a cab. The streets were filled with dancing, singing, music, people too jubilant to wait for the evening fiesta. We walked, dodging the jumping figures, keeping close to the market stalls that displayed "native" handicrafts im-

ported from New Jersey to Singapore to Grand La-
Clare.

Between the market and the hotel stretched a row
of business buildings and beyond them curved a shell
drive circling in to the hotel front entrance. The lobby was unexpectedly large, framed by glass-faced
shops, with the casino archway to the right. I started
toward the desk but Tara dug a key out of her bag.
She had already registered for me. We worked out
way through the tourists to the elevator and rode to
the top floor.

Tara led me to a suite, a big one facing the bay. I
looked down on a wide palm-studded lawn, a white
beach, sail boats dotting the green and blue water.
Money. Lots of it everywhere you looked. After the
night flight and the jail I felt too dirty to even sit on
the rich furniture. I went through the bedroom and
the bath. The shower was big enough for two. I
called to Tara.

"Bring fresh clothes and let's get clean."

"Oh, no," her laugh came back. "Not on an empty
stomach. My suite's next door and I'll wash there."

Well, I tried. I heard the connecting door open and
close, headed for the phone to ask room service for
drinks, then stripped and got under the water. I lux-
uriated in the hot flood until I was red, then switched
to cold. It made a new man of me even without sleep.
I was dressed by the time Tara came back in a low-
cut, clinging dress that matched her startling blue
eyes. Room service knocked as I reached for her.

The Martinique punch came in tall frosted glasses,
smooth and treacherous, but it didn't change her

mind so we finished them and rode the elevator down. Of the four hotel restaurants Tara chose the second floor terrace. We had a table under a bright umbrella and she told me the langoustes here were famous, dressed with butter and lime juice.

I wondered what was coming next, when the Russians would make their next move. I'd foiled their attempt at removing Fleming to safekeeping in a Cuban jail, so now they'd have to come up with a new program

But there was no sense going hungry while I waited for the counter-move. We ate a leisurely lunch, then walked arm in arm to Government House for Fleming's returning speech.

FOUR

Our timing was close. Every seat except our reserved ones was already taken and the hall was hot with too many bodies. Randolph Fleming sat on the speaker's platform flanked by the head of the legislative body on one side and the empty chair of Carib Jerome on the other. The Colonel stood at a microphone winding up a paean to the new president.

When he finished and Fleming stood, the walls nearly came down under the applause. I clapped too and Tara beat her hands together, her eyes damp with the joy of the moment.

Fleming waited smiling through fifteen minutes of ovation until the bedlam subsided enough so he could cut it off with a lift of his hands. When he could be heard, his voice rolled warm through the mike. He was humble at the welcome, grateful to be home, proud that Jerome had called on him to lead the country again. He outlined a program that made sense and promised an open election within one year so that he shouldn't continue in office by the present military decree. He spoke for an hour, giving a better political speech than most I had endured.

Another long ovation followed, with a cordon of soldiers keeping the crowd from rushing Fleming.

Then an escort took the three men on the stand off by a rear door. So far the army was sticking to its deal with Sawyer. I thought that in the face of the over-obvious popular approval, they'd run into trouble if they didn't keep their word. Tara and I waited until the crush around the door thinned. She had stars in her eyes.

"How about that, Nick? You know what Dr. Fleming did? General Hammond's family is still living in the palace. Fleming told them to take their time deciding where they'd go. He's staying at the hotel, has the whole floor just beneath us."

Somebody somewhere liked me. It would have taken some doing to keep an eye on Fleming in the presidential palace when I was masquerading as a hotel flunky. This put him in the middle of my supposed sphere. Then it dawned on me.

"You wouldn't happen to have nudged him into this, would you?"

Her smile said yes. She was a neat little conspirator herself.

"Fine," I told her. "I've got an excuse to look in on him, thank him for that assist out of the cooler."

The way was cleared and we left, Tara hugging my arm.

"And now that duty is done. . . ."

"You muffed your chance, lady. Duty isn't done and my afternoon is full. I'll walk you to the hotel—that's all." The only way to handle a tease is to tease back, so now Tara could whistle for a while. And there really were things I had to do—establish my cover with the hotel manager, call on Fleming, get some sleep. I'd had no rest in thirty-six hours and there was a heavy night ahead.

She was suspicious when I put her off, pouting when I put her in the elevator. Fair enough. I looked up the manager and found him in a huff too. He wasn't happy at having me on his staff, as though I were a reflection of poor performance on his part. He rang for his own security chief, Lewis, announced that Mr. Sawyer's new gentleman had finally arrived, and turned us out of his office.

Lewis was a huge black man who had played professional football in the United States a few years back. He was aloof until I called him Freight Train, the tab the press had hung on him, and recalled some of his big plays. Then he loosened up, told me about the special precautions he was taking with the President in residence, and took me up to Fleming's floor to introduce me to his staff.

There were four, all burly American blacks, huddled in a corner of the corridor. Lewis swore under his breath and growled about army arrogance. All alike, he said, everywhere, push you off the earth. He was burned because a lieutenant and two privates were by the doctor's door and had brushed off his guards. They had also apparently brushed off two men now languishing at a corridor intersection down the other way—swarthy, short, thick Italian-Americans. They gave me pause. The Mafia was looking out for the doctor too, protecting their own interests in the casino.

I was introduced to the hotel's security squad, then

to the three army men in front of Fleming's suite. I asked the lieutenant if the President was back. He looked through me without an answer. Lewis bellowed that I was Thomas Sawyer's handpicked man, imported to protect the doctor and they'd damn well better cooperate. The lieutenant still didn't see me; he just turned and knocked a code on the door. A flunky opened it. Fleming saw me from across the room and called for me to come in.

A swarm of government people filled the room, fighting for the great man's ear, with Colonel Jerome hovering nearest. I didn't stay long, only the minutes it took to thank Fleming and compliment him on his speech. Fleming was up to his ears organizing his government, but he was still solicitious of my welfare. He hoped I'd encounter no further difficulties on the island. I thanked him and left.

In the hall Lewis asked if I wanted to look at the security setup on the other floors. We rode down a flight and I saw soldiers, guards, Mafia everywhere. President Randolph Felming was tucked in tight.

I congratulated Lewis, excused myself and went into my room. The little booby traps I had left weren't disturbed. Nobody had been there. I wondered if AXE's information about the unreliability of the Grand LaClare army came from the fertile imagination of some nervous diplomat. I put in a call to headquarters to talk to David Hawk.

His voice lunged through the instrument, demanding to know why I hadn't reported in as soon as we landed. When he heard about the hassle over the gun, he had some special words for pompous officials, and

when he got that out of his system, I gave him a rundown on where else I'd been that had used up time.

"The skyjacking was set up by the Russians,
I'm sure," I said, "But that's all taken care of. The
stewardess didn't know she was a cat's paw. She's
not very bright, and she panicked. Do something for
her."

He was silent while he made a note, then, "Fleming, did he have any suspicion why you were aboard?
He's not stupid."

"He doesn't seem to realize why I'm around. Anyway, all is well on the island so far. The people act
like God is the new president."

"Splendid. Let's see how our Red friends react to
that. Keep your eyes open."

I blew a kiss at the mouthpiece, rang off, and went
for the Scotch room service had brought up with the
earlier drinks. I had two long, leisurely shots to toast
the chief. Then I phoned the desk to call me at five
and sacked out.

My face was set in a stiff smile when the ring
woke me. I took the luxury of a full yawn, called
Tara to meet me in the bar at five-thirty, and spent
most of the time until then in the shower. Vacation.

She had martinis in icy glasses waiting when I got
there, with every eye in the dim room undressing
her. Gorgeous. She was out to make me slaver and I
obliged. We dawdled over a few drinks. She knew a
restaurant at the far end of Bay Street with a terrace overlooking the harbor. We had turtle soup to
begin with, but I was too wrapped up in her to notice
the rest of what we ate.

Lights came on with the dusk like stars and formed a glittering necklace around the shore. From the street came the noise of wild celebrating.

"Let's go join them," I said.

A band was whooping it up at the open market and the mob was drunk on the joy of living, the air electric as a storm. The people dancing in such abandon were poor, descendants of slaves, ill used most of their lives. But there was a spark in them that hadn't been extinguished by the poverty of generations.

We danced all the way back to the hotel. On the top floor the sentries had been changed, but my hotel ID card cleared us. Without a word Tara stopped at my door. I opened it, held her back while I looked for signs of entry as a matter of habit, saw none and ushered her in.

Tara kicked off her shoes and wriggled long slender toes in the deep carpet while I poured warm whiskey for us. She tasted hers, tipped her head back and let it trickle down her throat.

"Now," she said, "I'll take you up on that offer of a shower."

On Grand LaClare you couldn't take too many. We went to the bedroom to undress and she had the advantage over me. She peeled off the little dress and there were no clothes underneath. I got out of my stuff, watching her. She had a long, lithe, golden body.

She walked ahead of me to the shower, turned the water on full, a little warmer than tepid, and stepped in. The space measured about four by six feet. We could have waltzed there. She didn't mind her hair getting wet, stood facing me, then moved to let the stream reach my body. I lathered my hands and soaped her, face, throat, body, feet.

I sudsed myself to a thick froth, and reached for her. She came against me, slippery, in a flow of movement.

Turning together to rinse off, I bent my head, found her mouth, kissed her, gently, slowly, and felt her respond.

I picked her up, snaring a large beach towel from the rack on my way to the bedroom. I smothered Tara in the towel, dropped it on the floor, then placed her gently on the king-sized bed. She was very ready when I lay down next to her. I entered her in one swift movement and she thrust up to meet me.

She was fantastic, anticipating me, joining me at every turn. I don't know how long we stayed together, but I fell asleep almost as soon as we finished. She had simply worn me out.

FIVE

We breakfasted in bed, Tara on tropical fruits, me on oysters, two dozen of them. I was still lingering over my meal when she finished and left me for a shower and fresh clothes in her suite. I had the whole day to play.

I was in the shower myself when the faint ring of the phone came through the noise in the stall. I tried to ignore it, but the caller was insistent. Made me think of Hawk. I left the water running and dripped across to the instrument.

The whispery voice from the receiver sounded conspiratorial. "Good morning, Mr. Carter. This is Carib Jerome. May I call on you for a few minutes?"

Well, yes. I'd been warned about Jerome by AXE; he could be the Russians' man on the island. Or it could be simply a protocal visit and I shouldn't offend him.

"Give me ten to dress," I said.

I called room service for hot coffee and another cup, turned off the shower, toweled down, strapped on the sheath with the stiletto, got into clean clothes and was buttoning the jacket over the holster when the Colonel and the coffee arrived. My mind had been reviewing what Hawk had given me on the man.

Jerome was thirty-six years old, a member of a prominent Out Island family. Educated at Oxford.

With a special course at Sandhurst. Came home after school, joined the native constabulary and made a name as a law officer. When Randolph Fleming was first elected president and the British troops left, Parliament thought Grand LaClare needed an army of its own. The doctor had appointed the chief of police—Hammond—general of the new force and made Jerome chief of staff.

Hawk had said: "The Colonel surprised us. CIA had him tabbed as politically ambitious and looked for a power grab by him when Hammond went down. Instead Jerome immediately asked Fleming to come back."

The AXE think tank had speculated on his motives. Why did an ambitious man, who had the opportunity to put himself into power, call instead on the one opponent he had helped run off the island? Our experts thought Jerome was intelligent enough to recognize his own unpopularity, to realize that the Parliament would fight him. That he believed if he put Fleming in as president, he could make himself the strong man behind the throne.

I had asked Hawk if Jerome had any idea of my real identity. He didn't. As far as he was concerned, I was only Thomas Sawyer's representative.

The Colonel came through the door ahead of the coffee boy and stood rigid, unsmiling, until we were alone. Only his dark eyes moved. They scurried. Through the open bedroom door. To the big bed with the covers on the floor. To the Scotch and glasses on the bureau. He made a long study of me as I brought him coffee, black. Still no smile.

I decided on caution. The door closed behind the boy. Jerome settled himself in a deep chair and tasted his brew.

"Nice quarters," the husky voice said without inflection. But there was a question somewhere in it.

I should have thought of it when I first saw the suite. This was VIP country. What was a hotel cop doing here? I passed an admiring, envious look at the expensive furnishings and tried a short laugh.

"How the upper class suffer. I get one taste of it because the hotel's full. They'll have me in the basement soon."

At that season, the place would be full and the Colonel would know it. In countries like Grand La-Clare, hotels must file their guest lists with the police.

"Pity." He held my eyes. Then he raised his brows and dropped the subject. "I wanted this opportunity to thank you in person for aborting the hijack. Extremely fortunate for President Fleming—and for me—that you were aboard. And armed." A puzzled frown. "Was it known that you carried a gun on the plane?"

I didn't blink. Gave him a smile that shared a secret. "My employer knows I like my own tools. He has some influence."

"Of course." His first smile came then, brought forth by the thought of my special privilege. "Again, fortunate. President Fleming would be dead today, or in Communist hands, but for your quick thinking. You must be a very accomplished security officer to react so rapidly."

It was a question. How much more than a hotel dick was I? I stayed cautious.

"I was escorting Miss Sawyer. She could've been hurt or killed, and my reflexes react when a gun is aimed toward me."

"Oh?" Was that really surprise? "You weren't aware our president was the target? But, of course, in your position you could not know he was going to be kidnapped to Cuba."

"Is that a fact?" I sounded incredulous. "Did the stewardess confess the plot?"

His eyes, his hoarse voice were flat. "We have the information from other sources. The girl escaped before I had the time to question her."

Escaped from the jail I'd been in? I thought about scared little dupe. Or was she an agent, good enough to sell me that act? Jerome appeared to read my mind.

"Her innocence act took the matron in. She used karate, knocked the woman out, stole her clothes and simply walked away."

We were on an island with an abundance of police. I said, "Where could she go?"

An impatient shrug. "Cruise boats come and go. I understand she was artful enough to have won her way aboard one of them."

It was hard for me to buy. But then I wouldn't have believed a stewardess could bring a pair of guns on a plane. The Colonel waved the incident out of mind and sank back, complacent.

"No matter, really. Thanks to you our president arrived safely and is taking up the reins of govern-

ment. The army is convined it is in its best interest
to give Dr. Fleming its full support, so our problems
are resolved to everyone's satisfaction. I hope your
transition into the job here will be as smooth as
ours." He finished the coffee and stood up. "If I can
help you with anything, you'll find me at the Palace."

I took the hand he offered and saw him to the door.
He knew more about me than he'd admitted. That
was clear from his assurance to me that the lid was
on the army. Simple gratitude about the skyjacking
didn't require that he discuss political maneuverings
with a hotel dick. I suspected he was telling me that
the undercover job was no longer necessary.

I gave him time to get clear of the hotel, then left
the room. The soldiers were gone from the top floor.
So were Lewis' men. But the Mafia boys still pored
over the racing form beside the elevators.

I dropped down to Fleming's floor. Only the syndicate's crowd was represented. They said the doctor
was still asleep. I walked down to the next flight and
found the same personnel. Strange.

I decided it was time to move on to my next stop.
The Casino. I was looking for some answers and they
might be there.

Roulette tables, faro banks, and crap tables made a
rectangle around the pit, connected by velvet
wrapped chains. No one except the dealers and pit
bosses was allowed inside. Only the chained-off area
offered a modicum of clear space. The rest of the
floor crawled with humanity.

There were no windows beckoning to the outdoors.
No clocks to tick off time. There was only the clatter

of chips and glasses and hoarse pleadings that dice, balls, cards fall this way or that. Not my kind of gambling. Mine is a bet every day that when I get out of bed in the morning, I'll make it back in one piece at night.

Trying to make my way through this raucous crowd, I got bogged down in the crush of milling flesh as it stampeded toward a jackpot winner. Bells rang for the lucky dope, singled out as a come-on to keep the other slots hot. Bells rang for me too. A redhead stood ten feet away, lips curled in scorn, brows arched at the madness.

She stood out like a spotlight. Five nine or ten, sleek shining nipple-length hair, a pantsuit swelled in all the right places.

While I waited for the herd to pass, the space around her cleared. She turned and escaped to the uncrowded pocket around the cashiers' cages, paused at the end grille for an instant, then shoved open an unmarked door and went through. I was headed that way myself. She added urgency to my visit.

A man whose luck held beat me to the cage. I waited while the clerk racked the chips, then shoved stacked silver to the winner. When the man moved off, the clerk flicked a look at my empty hands and said in a bored voice, "Help you, friend?"

I don't like being called friend by someone I never saw in my life. "Chip Cappola. I want to see him."

The blank face went blanker. "Never heard of him."

I put my new ID card on the counter. It said I was security chief for the Sawyer Grand LaClare. The swarthy clerk sneered and gave me empty eyes. "Why didn't you say so?"

"You didn't ask. Mr. Sawyer expects courtesy to the guests from the staff. What's your name?"

He didn't like that. But he was the sort of bully who deflates when authority's pin sticks him.

"Tony Ricco." It was a mumble.

I said, "You get one warning. Not a second. Don't let me hear a complaint. Now, Cappola."

"Right through this door." He was in a helpful sweat now, indicating the way the redhead had gone, buzzing the electric lock under his counter.

The thick metal door folded back on silent hinges at my shove. I went through to a blind passage. Back here the building looked like a vault and was used as one. A huge black man sat at a desk studded with un- identified buttons along its back edge. He wore a khaki uniform, no insignia, and could have been ei- ther island or hotel police. He was just as cordial as the cashier. The cold eyes watched me come toward him.

I said, "Cappola," and dropped the ID.

He bent toward a speaker that was set flush in the desk, flicked the switch, and said in a deep growl, "A Mr. Carter. New security guy."

An answer grated back, fuzzed by the intercom. "Shoot him through."

The man dipped his head, thumbed a button and a panel across the corridor slid aside without sound. Beyond it was a large room, with bare yellow walls, a desk with nothing on it, some empty chairs and a deep couch with the redhead draped against its back. A cigarette set in her mouth, sending blue smoke in a thin straight rise past half-lowered eyes. She showed no surprise to see me.

Chip Cappola tilted his chair back behind the desk, looking like George Raft hoped he did thirty years ago. Dark straight oiled hair plastered flat, deep olive skin over a tight face that was still sleek but would be creviced and jowly in a few years. The coat of his white silk suit hung on a hanger against the wall. His lavender shirt with a maroon monogram on the sleeve was the bright spot in the drab room. His tone was drab too.

"The geese came south early this year."

"They didn't stop in Miami," I told him.

I don't know who dreams up the recognition signals we use to make a new contact. They're supposed to sound innocuous and yet not likely to have been spoken by accident, although agents have been known to make mistakes with outsiders. Cappola looked me up and down, a sardonic twist on his brown lips.

"Nick Carter, huh? Killmaster, huh? You don't look like any hit man I ever saw. That kind of job takes guts."

I winked at the redhead and asked him, "You like to inspect mine?"

He shrugged. "Not unless you got 'em with polka dots. You see one, you seen them all."

The girl chortled, and the man at the desk threw a thumb her way "Mitzy Gardner there. Maybe you heard of her."

I had indeed. But she wasn't the Mitzy type. She

was a bomb, and notorious in her own right. Her rap sheet said she'd been mistress to a long list of top echelon hoods, four of them now dead. An educated guess put her as a bag girl for all of them, trusted to carry Mafia money to Miami, to be moved on to the Bahamas for laundering before it went to Swiss bank accounts.

Chip Cappola now headed her list, a man high in gangster ranks, wanted in the States and unable to go to the mainland. It was a laugh that with his record he was presently up to his thick neck working for AXE.

Cappola wasn't interested in national security. His loyalty was exclusively to the nation of the underworld. But he decidedly did not want the Communists taking this casino away from him and so it was to his advantage to have Randolph Fleming as president. With Fleming in the saddle, Cappola's business on Grand LaClare could continue as it had under Hammond.

Cappola waved at a chair and I took it. He said, "I'm damned glad you lucked in on the flight with Fleming. We lose him, we'll get our throats cut. The casino goes down the drain and Sawyer's out another hotel." There was undisguised worry in the flat, rasping voice.

"We didn't loose him," I reminded the gangster. "He's president and Colonel Jerome says everything's quiet."

The front legs of his chair hit the floor hard. "You talked to Jerome? Tell him who you are?" He spat the words out. There was fury in his voice.

I said. "Why are you so mad?"

"Did you tell him?"

"Of course not. What have you got against him?"

He put both hands flat on the desk and leaned over them. "Carib Jerome ordered Fleming kidnapped."

I kept a straight face. "What gave you that idea, Cappola?"

"Idea? We *know*. You think nobody but AXE keeps track of what's what? We got an ear in Cuba. He's like this with Fidel." He held up two fingers tight together. "Jerome wants Fleming out of the way for good."

"Uh-uh." I wasn't impressed. Whatever information the Cosa Nostra had, it didn't match with ours nor did it fit with the Colonel's behavior. "Fleming was out of the way in the States. Jerome called him back."

Cappola had a wicked grin. "Because you pulled the rug. Listen to me, buster. As long as Fleming was loose on the mainland, Jerome couldn't make his power play and bring the Reds in here. The U.S. would have put the Doc in the front boat, shipped him over and supervised the election. Jerome would've been booted off the island. But with Fleming in a Cuban jail, Jerome could yell that if he was running the country, he could bail out the Doc. He'd be put in the Palace in a blink and that would be the last anybody ever heard of Randolph Fleming."

I'll listen to anything that makes sense. What Cappola was saying might. But I wasn't jumping on the Mafia bandwagon yet. Even if all this was true, Jerome's hands were tied now.

A buzzer sounded like a snake, three quick hisses. Cappola rammed to his feet, read the doubt in my face, and said across my shoulder to the redhead, "Take him out of circulation and tell him the rest of it." He went out of the office fast.

Mitzy Gardner got off the couch and slung a bag over her shoulder without hurry, watching me, appraising, mocking.

"Heart attack in the casino," she said without interest. "Happens once in awhile, a big winner or a big loser." She had a scorching voice that came clear from her chest. "Let's take a ride, lover."

"The security chief walk out on trouble? If you really think Jerome made a try for Fleming, it's my job to see a second grab doesn't come off."

She shrugged lightly. "The casino has its own staff apart from the hotel's. Fleming's safe for the day. Chip has him bottled up in bed, doped. He's not going anywhere and you need to hear and see a few things."

She touched the door control and led me through, telling the black lackey with easy familiarity, "We're going down, Duke."

He stretched a white grin for her. Liked her looks better than mine. The button he chose opened an elevator at the opposite end of the hall from the casino entrance. It took us to a four-car basement garage with a Volks station wagon and a long lavender Cadillac. Nice privacy for visitors who didn't want to be seen. I commented on that.

Her smile was wry. "The elevator goes to Chip's roof penthouse too. That's where Fleming is."

She slid under the wheel of the Caddy. I sat beside her.

"On the floor until we clear the hotel," she told me. "Jerome would have a tail on you if you showed."

I played along, let her try to spook me, doubled down on the floor as she pushed a button. A steel partition sighed up. She kicked the big motor to life and we purred under the door. The hollow echo beyond indicated a larger garage with the grease smell of a service section, then we nosed up a ramp to ground level. The shell drive whispered under the tires. She made the turn toward town at the boulevard and half a mile later beckoned me up. The litter from yesterday's celebration was being swept up and the street was back to its normal quiet.

"Jerome," I said. "If there was anything to Cappola's suspicion, the obvious way to remove Fleming would have been to kill him. Why send him to Cuba?"

She didn't even glance at me. "A corpse is of no use to anyone. Fleming alive might be used as a bargaining point against Russia."

"Possibly. Now about me, why would Jerome want a tail on me?"

Her look withered me. "He stumbled over you once. That business with your gun didn't just happen. He wanted you out. How many times do you have to be hit on the head to wise up?"

I put it all on the back burner to cook. With Fleming safely in Cappola's cocoon for the coming hours, there was time to think ahead and plan moves, things best done in relaxation. I relaxed.

We drove past the open market and through Government Park where the Palace dominated. Beyond that, alone on a hilltop, crouched a great time-blackened fort from the early days. Its base would be honeycombed with dungeons for government prisoners. Ugly place. At the bottom of the hill on the bay side was the cluster of the old town. The road narrowed there. Mitzy crawled past donkeys, carts, native women in bright skirts and kerchiefs toting loads on top of their heads. The color, old charm and history of the island was on parade here, where tourists didn't venture.

The houses petered out. Mountains rose from the side of the highway away from the water. Against the bay, in lonely isolation, an old resort hotel rotted away silently. Gingerbread dripped from roofs and balconies, wide verandas sagged into the blooming lawn gone wild in a tangled riot. Doors and windows were boarded with plywood. In Victoria's time it had been elegant.

"The old Poinciana," the redhead said. "Finest place in the Caribbean when it was built. Termite paradise now. I looked at it once for a Miami friend with a notion he could revitalize it. Huh-uh. But it's still used. The mountain people camp there when they want to stay near town."

A couple of things about her seemed odd. She didn't speak like a moll. Her well-modulated voice held intelligence and breeding. And for a mere bag girl, her opinions appeared to carry weight among the Mafia. She was obviously something more than a carrier of unlawful money. She had even been told my true identity. That made me curious. I asked her how come. She gave me a Mona Lisa smile.

"When Chip got scared he could lose the casino, I called Davey and told him to shoot you down here for the rescue."

Davey? *Davey* Hawk?

Hawk taking orders from this broad? It hit me right between the eyes. Was Mitzy Gardner an AXE agent? Was Hawk playing games, letting me dig it out by myself?

"Honey," I said, "fun and games are fine, but who the hell are you?"

My question got a counter question. "Which one of my hats would you like me to put on?"

I damned her under my breath and leered to even the score. "I'd rather see you take them all off."

She didn't lose her cool. "You're in luck. We're on our way"

We continued into open country with jungle growing thick down to the road on both sides. Then there were patches of sugar cane and small banana plantations. The girl talked about the changing economy of the place. Bananas brought more profit than sugar cane—green gold she called them. Mace, cloves, cinnamon, and the fragrant tonka beans were also becoming popular crops. She said she had a small plantation on the far side of the island. A nest egg for a rainy day I assumed.

The road was anything but straight. It followed the shore for awhile, then it bent toward the mountains that formed a spine down the middle of the island.

When the plantations were behind us, the ground roughened into swamp jungle on the sea side and wrinkled into hogbacks and canyons the other way, heavily timbered and tangled with vine. We were about twelve miles from town when Mitzy swung the heavy car away from the road into two sand ruts, wallowed a quarter of a mile down that and stopped where the trees did, at the back of a lagoon.

She killed the engine, kicked out of her sandals, and opened her door. I sat admiring the view. The shore cupped around deep blue water to a horn half a mile away. There the land rose abruptly to a high nose with the hint of an ancient fortification still visible.

The view in front of me was even better. Mitzy was out of the Caddy, running, shucking off jacket and pants, briefs, streaking for the water. She turned and flung an arm to wave at me. I didn't need a second invitation. I dropped my own clothes and went after her, but she'd had a head start and hit the water well before I did.

There was only a low swell of lazy surf and the lagoon was warm as new drawn milk. The girl struck off with a strong, fluid stroke and was far from shore when I caught up with her. I couldn't touch bottom but we treaded. Her skin was sleek under my hands. I reached for her hips to pull her to me. She flung herself backward, her body sinking and circled her legs around me. Neither of us was quite ready when she raised her head and gasped, using her arms in a stroke to drive herself on me.

In that deep water I had no leverage. I didn't need

it. She had enough for both of us. Her timing was great.

When it was over, she loosened her legs, and floated to the surface. I floated up beside her and we rested. In the warm stillness I went to sleep. I didn't know it until my head went under and I swallowed lukewarm salt water.

The girl was gone. Sputtering, I looked around. She was lying on the beach on her stomach, brown against the white sand, her back unmarked by swimsuit patches. I swam in, stretched out beside her and went to sleep again. The next thing I knew her throaty voice was saying, "Rise and shine, Carter. You're about to meet a friend."

I clawed back to consciousness. The sun was low in the west. I couldn't see anyone on the beach except the pair of us. Nothing moved but a few sluggish crabs. Then she pointed along the cove toward the headland. Something was advancing across the water, and it wasn't a boat.

It looked like a human figure. I was groggy but not that groggy. I blinked, shook my head and looked again. It was still there. A thousand feet away and out at the depth where I hadn't been able to find footing, a man was walking. Tall, blue-black, thin, in a long white robe that billowed out like dry cloth. He came toward us dignified but purposeful. It was unbelievable.

The girl stood up casually and waved, went to gather her clothes and got into them without hurry.

Was it voodoo? Or had she mainlined me with valium while I was out? I knew it was hallucination. I knew the cove water was salty. Floating on it was easy. I knew it felt like syrup. But even so it didn't keep me from sinking when I fell asleep on it.

The man kept coming. About ten feet from the shore, he lifted his robe to his waist, above a twist of loincloth, sank slowly in the water to his thighs and rose again in a stride up the beach.

He looked to be seven feet tall. He was old and his long beard and hair were white. His frame was skinny, but taut with muscle.

I sat naked on the sand and I looked up at the high brow, the somber eyes, the wide mouth that smiled at Mitzy Gardner. She was beside me again and he took her hand in fingers that would span a basketball, holding it gently as if it were an uncooked egg. She spoke to him in a language I didn't know and they laughed. She looked down at me and said in English, "Meet Noah, Nick. He's lived here since heaven knows when. And he's another who doesn't want Red missiles on his island."

I stood up. What else?

Noah studied me, lingering on my middle section, then offered a hand. Mine disappeared in his palm, but his pressure was only enough to be a solid, honest grip. It was real flesh I touched, warm, with blood inside, alive.

"My admiration, Mr. Carter." The accent was impeccably British, the tone a muted baritone that would thunder if he chose. "Mitzy claims accomplishments for you that strain my credulity."

"*Your* credulity?" I swallowed. "At least what I do is possible. I'm afraid you're impossible to believe."

His eyes went to Mitzy and held hers. There was a

bond between them, a bond of respect, friendship, understanding. Then he brought his attention back to me.

"I must apologize, Mr. Carter. I asked Mitzy to bring you before you became too involved with your duties. Unhappily, a problem has developed up there." He gestured toward the mountain. "There is a serious illness I must exorcize. I will not be able to stay now, but I felt I should meet you at least and promise you our help should you need it. You will visit me again, I hope."

He bent, kissed the girl's forehead lightly, nodded to me, walked back to the shore, hiked up his robe, waded out, stepped up to the surface and walked away across the water.

I gawked after him. Mitzy giggled.

"What happened to your cool? The egg on your face is drying."

I pointed after the apparition. "How?"

She sobered, gave me a long, speculative look and said, "Don't question too much, Nick. I've seen some very unsettling things since I met that man. You will too. Now we'd better get back to Fleming before he wakes up and wants to hit the street."

I got into my clothes. Slowly. I kept watching the tall black figure until it disappeared among the rocks at the base of the hill.

"Give," I told the girl. "What's the story on your friend?"

She lifted a brown shoulder. "You heard me before. Just be prepared for surprises. Noah's full of them and I'm sure I haven't seen or heard them all."

She ran away from me toward the car. The engine roared, full-throated, before I got there. As soon as I was in the seat, she spun the wheels on the hard sand and headed out to the road.

I didn't for one minute buy the story that Noah had some special magic up his sleeve. He struck me as particularly sane and shrewd.

"Is he a hermit?" I asked Mitzy.

"Anything but. He rules a tribe of over a hundred people up in that old fort. He says his people hold up there a couple of hundred years ago, after a slave rebellion. They're a spooky lot. They can be all around you in the jungle and you won't see one unless he intends you to."

"How did you get acquainted?"

The full lips pursed and she faced me. "Funny about that, too. I was at the cove for a swim one day and he came down to give me a message. Chip's second in command at the casino had been shot and Chip was looking for me to take the word to Miami. The guy was killed at 3:10 in the afternoon. It was a quarter after three when Noah told me."

That was easier. I was back on solid ground. "Jungle drums." I laughed. "Bamboo telegraph."

"Probably. But later I saw him cure a very sick woman with voodoo. He claimed to have exorcised her devils into the sea. She got up right away."

My scalp prickled. The girl beside me was tough enough to survive in the tough world of the Mafia. That takes pragmatism. Now she was talking about voodoo and black magic, almost believing it. I didn't ask any more questions.

We rode in silence for five miles. Suddenly there was a black man standing in the middle of the road, a hand raised to stop us. Mitzy pulled up beside him. He sounded excited; she asked him something in the native dialect and he shook his head. She looked worried, whipped the car in reverse, made a U-turn and kicked the accelerator to the floor.

"Noah wants us in a hurry," she said. "Something's happened, but he didn't say what."

I glanced at her, then looked back toward the messenger. The road was empty. When we passed the next turn, the road deteriorated badly and we should've had a jeep to bounce up that climb. I winced for the Caddy. Halfway to the top, the track ended at a pothole two feet deep.

"We walk from here," the girl said.

We didn't exactly walk. We clambered like mountain goats through the trees. We came out of the timber at a high wall built of limestone.

The fortress covered the whole headland and looked impregnable. Beyond the gate the courtyard was set in the same limestone. Stone buildings backed against the wall faced inward, some crumbling but others in good condition, forming a platform with their roofs.

The population was gathered around Noah. They were very dark with Indian faces, men in loincloths, women wearing only short, brilliant skirts, naked spidery children, all silent and solemn.

Noah came through them as we walked in, his face grave, drawn, his eyes fierce.

Without preamble he gave it to us. "Dr. Fleming

has been kidnapped. Chip Cappola was killed trying to prevent it. Jerome has occupied the hotel. All Americans and Europeans on the island are being evacuated on the cruise boats."

"Where's Tara Sawyer?" I asked.

Not until later did it dawn on me that I had simply accepted the information out of hand. Through my silent five-mile ride with Mitzy, I had heard not a single beat of drums.

"The message did not mention her," Noah told me.

At least there had been a message. He wasn't conjuring up visions.

I said, "How did you hear about this?"

He cast a look at the people crowding around us and his lips turned up at the corners.

"Do not doubt me, Mr. Carter, there is not time. The doctor is being held in the dungeons under the old fort and must be rescued. Your Miss Sawyer is probably being sent home on one of the boats."

"Not likely. I can't see Jerome letting her go when he could hold up her father for ransom."

"You have a point there. There is other news. Descriptions of you both have been broadcast and a reward, a thousand dollars each, is offered for your capture."

I swore aloud. "I go joyriding and the sky falls down. . . ."

"As well you did," Noah interrupted. "Had you been in the hotel, you would be dead now and could do nothing. As it is, you can fight."

"Well, I'd better do something." I touched the girl. "Stay here; you'll be safe. I'll borrow the car."

"No dice. You don't know the territory. I do and I'm on this job, too." There was a metallic hardness in her voice, a hint of the strength that had gouged her a place in the Brotherhood.

"She is right," Noah backed her up. "You cannot return to Port of Spain by the coast road. Jerome has it blocked. You'll have to go through the mountains and you'll need help." He pointed a long finger at one squat, dark man, then another. "Pants. Shirts. Guide them."

The men ran for the buildings.

While we waited, Noah added, "They speak English and are intelligent. Go down to the car and they will meet you there."

I didn't like this. How did I know Noah's story was true? And who wanted his escorts on a trip that could end God knew where? But I had no choice. I was outnumbered by Noah's boys and even Mitzy was on his side. So I went along—at least for now.

By the time we reached the Caddy, the pair were there, grinning. Our guides now wore knee-length white cotton pants and white shirts with the sleeves torn out. Machetes were stuck under their rope belts. They swung into the back seat of the car, giving directions.

There was enough turning room for a donkey cart. The girl rocked the car back and forth for five minutes before we were headed downhill. The main road had been bad. This one hardly existed. We took it in low gear over a Swiss cheese of holes, and for added pleasure came abruptly out of the trees on a sheer cliff on the far side of the mountain spine. We turned to follow a narrow lane downward. The fenders scraped the wall on one side and on the other I looked straight down to a canyon bottom. I didn't say a word—talking might distract Mitzy, who was driving.

There was half a mile of that, then we were in timber again with a fence of trunks on either side. I started breathing again.

"So you know the territory," I said to Mitzy. "How do we get into Jerome's dungeon?"

She shook her head. "We'll have to work on that. Our first stop should be that old resort hotel I showed you on our way to meet Noah. We can get ourselves together there and consolidate our plans."

I said it was O.K. with me and she drove towards Noah's hotel. It was getting dark when we reached a road wide enough for a car. We caught glimpses of lights below us through the trees so we were close to town. Mitzy flipped on the headlights to enter the highway.

The beam picked up a man in uniform with a rifle leveled on us. The girl hit the brakes fast, threw into reverse and backed up. On a hunch I looked behind the car. The rear lights showed another soldier raising a rifle. My Luger was up and blasting before his gun was high enough. At the same time the windshield exploded. Glass showered over the girl but she kept driving. Then I fired through the windshield frame and the man in front of the car fell.

Mitzy stopped the Caddy and I had time to look at our guides. They were crouched behind the front seat. I thought they might have been hit by the shots,

but both of them straightened. They'd been frightened—and cautious. I got out for the presents Colonel Jerome had handed me. Both his soldiers were
dead. I took the uniforms, tossed them in the rear
seat, then brought in the rifles. Noah's men grabbed
them like professionals.

I said, "You know how those work?"

They did. They'd been in the palace guard when
Fleming was president. That knowledge might come
in handy some time. For now, I hung onto the weapons while they dragged the bodies into the brush and
left them for whatever hungry cat came along.

The roadblock proved Noah's information. There
was more to the old man than I'd been willing to admit. So Jerome had taken over, just like Noah'd said.
I'd better get my thinking gear together and figure
out a way to free Fleming. Noah's credibility also
gave me new faith in his guides. Since they'd signed
up for the trip anyway, and since they could handle
firearms, they might come in handy later, when I had
to face-down Colonel Jerome.

We made the hotel without being jumped again and
Mitzy pulled the Caddy into a ramshackle shed at the
back. We went from there to the broken-down lobby.

Mildew and rotting wood stank up the air. Our
guides crossed the lobby floor and led us down stairs
that creaked and sagged, into the kitchen, a big one
with a long wood range against one wall and a work
table in the middle. We were not alone. A candle
burned on the table and three black men were eating
an iguana, a delicacy that made my empty stomach
snarl.

There was a lot of fast talking, the exhibiting of the guns and uniforms, congratulations all around, and, finally, introductions. When all the hands were shaken, I found a pan of water in the sink, rinsed the blood off the uniform fronts, then joined the supper party. With the edge off my hunger, I felt a little less like a yoyo at the end of a string of astonishments and disasters. My plate was still half full when the three tribesmen left. I was thankful to see them go. We had battle plans to go over and I didn't relish unwanted company.

Noah had given me our guides' names when we first got together, but since I didn't know the language, I couldn't remember them. It seemed to me they ran long, with a great many syllables. I didn't want to offend these men by calling them Tom or Harry, so I explained the problem and asked for help.

The taller one laughed and said, "You can call me Lambie." He pronounced it with a hard "B."

Mitzy leaned close to my ear. "Lambie is a big salt-water conche. They eat the meat as an aphrodisiac."

"It has flair." I smiled. "Says a lot more than N3 by way of a nickname. And you?" I looked at the other guide.

His lips stretched wide. "Caco."

"Short enough," I approved. "What's that mean?"

He smiled. "A bird of prey. Very fierce."

"Fine." I beamed. They were sharp. And they could joke even in the face of taking on the whole island army. Maybe we had some kind of chance.

"You understand that we have to get inside that

prison, find Dr. Fleming and take him out alive. But
first we must get inside. Does anyone know of any
old escape routes prisoners may have dug in the
past?" I looked around.

The answer was no. There had been one. They described it. A slender mole hole that ran from a cell to
the face of the hill below the foundations. It had been
too narrow to turn around in and too steep to allow
anyone to crawl backwards to the cell. There was an
iron grille across the hillside where the passage
opened. A bleached skull pressed against the bars inside and finger bones still wrapped around them. So
much for that. I would have to play it by ear and it
could be messy.

I said so. "Are you ready to tackle it?"

I got two elaborate shrugs, fatalistic. Caco said
quietly. "If Fleming dies, we die anyway. Jerome
wants our mountain for his missile station. He will
come for it and we have not enough men and too few
weapons to stop him."

More and more I liked Noah's men. There was
no guessing their ages, but their skin was sleek, with
good muscle under it, and there was nothing wrong
with their coordination. They moved with the grace
of jungle cats. I pointed at the uniforms.

"Climb into those. You'll play the part of soldiers.
You've captured Mitzy and me and you'll deliver us
at the fort. You'll tell them Jerome has ordered us
locked in with Dr. Fleming, in the same cell."

The girl's eyes slitted. I didn't like putting her life
in jeopardy, but our "capture" would be more convincing if she was with us.

Caco and Lambie peeled out of the shirts and pants, hesitated over the loin clothes, then shyly turned their backs and unwound those. Both were wearing *ouanga,* battle charm sacks on thongs around their necks. Rifles were fine, but I guess they felt it didn't hurt to take along a little extra protection. They buttoned the uniform jackets over the charms, hiked up the army trousers, and squared to attention.

We went back through the tunnel to the shed. Mitzy still drove, with me beside her in front. The two men stood up in the rear with their rifles against our necks.

The girl backed out and headed for the fort, using rear alleys. Tonight the streets were empty, everyone keeping indoors behind drawn blinds. The shops were dark and barred against looters. Port of Spain was a silent, grim city, altogether different from the gay place of the night before.

We climbed toward the fort on the low hill. A green lawn in front of the building tried to make it look innocent, but the iron fence surrounding it and a cannon bristling midway spoiled the effect. So did the sentry box outside the fence.

A corporal and two privates saw our climbing lights and walked into the road with rifles ready. Mitzy slowed and stopped short of them. Behind me Lambie cried out:

"Corporal, come see what we have. The fat prize." He shoved my head forward with the rifle barrel, giving a high laugh.

The corporal came near with caution. Both our

boys broke into a hairy story of the battle they'd had
to take us. They made it good and convincing. The
corporal was impressed. While our guys were still
bragging, he raised his rifle, centering it on me.

My stomach tightened. He wouldn't shoot Mitzy, I
was sure, because of the possible ransom. But what
Jerome had in mind for me might be something else.
The corporal let me stew while he took the pleasure
of watching me through his sights. Then he barked a
command. The privates moved out of the road. The
corporal climbed into the rear seat and ordered Mitzy to drive up to the fort.

It was a grisly looking building, no windows and
only a single, center door like an open mouth. It
made me think of a blind beast that ate people who
displeased its master. It even had a plank tongue
protruding from it. Mitzy stopped on the paved park-
ing lot in front, and I saw that the planks were a
drawbridge across a moat. It was weed-choked now,
but in times past there would've been a line of slaves
hauling sea water to fill it. Any attack would've had
a wet crossing.

A private held the center of the bridge and the
whole area was floodlighted. Our corporal got out
and leveled his rifle again.

"Get them to the ground while I cover the man."

I was prodded again and stepped out. Mitzy got
out on the other side. Caco and Lambie kept their
guns in our backs. The corporal gloated for a bit,
then left us to cross the drawbridge and enter the
fort. Minutes later he strutted back with a lieutenant. The private on the bridge presented arms smart-

ly and the new man's austere bearing tipped me he was in command.

The corporal chattered with excited gestures, hopping around until the officer slashed a hand to shut him up. From the glitter in the lieutenant's eyes, I thought I knew who would collect Jerome's reward, if this had been the real capture.

Lambie said smartly, "Colonel's orders, sir. These two are to be locked up with Fleming. All the netted birds together."

"Understood," the lieutenant snapped. "Bring them into the guard room."

He about-faced and we were walked into the old building along a stone passage, a place of chill echoes, a nightmare for a claustrophobiac. In the guard room the lieutenant flicked a hand that ordered us searched.

Caco chirped, "We did that when we caught them, sir. Stripped them clear down."

"You did well." The lieutenant turned a smirk on me. "Nick Carter, is it. Very dangerous, the colonel said. Tonight your teeth are going to be pulled, I think."

I let my shoulders slump and put on a hangdog look. He swung his attention to Mitzy. Even with tears in her eyes and huddled like a frightened kitten she was a lot to see. Maybe he even liked her better submissive. His hips swayed and he pried her chin up with a forefinger.

"You, there. The colonel says you are valued by the Syndicate, that they will pay well to have you back. We will ask."

Mitzy cowered further, pressed a hand over her mouth and whimpered. "Please, sir, please don't send me there. They'll kill me."

The man's brows climbed. "If you have value, why would they do that?"

She chewed her lip, holding back, then as though she saw that he had the power to make her talk, she whispered, "I was carrying some money for them. I didn't deliver it. . . ."

Dollar signs pinwheeled in the dark eyes. He sounded eager. "Where is it now?"

Suddenly looking hopeful, her words pounced. "I could show you. I couldn't describe where. . . . But if you turn us loose, I'd. . . ."

His laugh was nasty. "No need for that, is there? As for Carter, the colonel would chain me in his place if I lost him." He shrugged. "For some reason, Jerome is very impressed."

The girl twisted her fingers together, held them toward the man, moved toward him, supplication and sensuousness in every step.

"Just me then? You and I?"

Lust lit up his face. Without taking his eyes off her, he spoke to our two men.

"One of you stay here, the other take Carter to the cell."

I had a bad minute while I thought the lieutenant meant to stay with the girl. Then I realized he was sending me below with a single guard. I moved a few muscles as if I liked the idea and would try to jump the guard along the way. I thought Mitzy could handle the officer all right, but there might be a fight,

noise, and I didn't want a fracas to bring in more soldiers. The lieutenant caught my movements, smirked,
and decided to go along with me, after all. He started
out the door ahead of me and Lambie. Mitzy called
after him, sugar sweet.

"Lieutenant. . . . I'll be waiting . . ."

He marched down the corridor more jaunty than
military. I glanced over my shoulder as we left. The
lieutenant's mind would not be entirely on duty while
he took me to the cell.

At the end of the hall he opened a door, a stone
slab, waved us ahead and pulled it closed after him.
With that granite shut tight, no sound from the dungeons would be heard above ground. We went down
a circular stone stairway to another passage. Down
here water dripped from limestone stalactites on the
arched ceiling, winking in the light of the officer's
lantern. There was no other illumination. He took
the lead again, past about twenty grilled doors on either side of the stinking passage. At the far end he
fished a brass key six inches long from a pocket, un-
locked the grille and preceded me into the cell.

Dr. Fleming was against the back wall, one knee
drawn up, the other leg stretched out badly swollen.
He was sitting on the green slime that covered the
stone floor, one hand held above his head by a thick
iron cuff on a chain stapled into the wall.

He raised his head, blinked against the light, saw
me at the edge of it and straightened. Then he saw
the guard with the rifle and finally, the lieutenant.

Fleming's shoulders dropped again and he let his
head fall. The officer stood above him, smiling. He

unbuttoned his holster, lifted out his gun and stepped aside where he could watch both Fleming and me, raising the gun slowly toward my middle.

"Doctor." The voice was oily. "Did you hope you had an effective ally on the island? A man who saved you once and might again? I present him to you now. I will leave him with you. After I have assured myself that he will stay here to answer Colonel Jerome's questions."

Behind me Lambie's breath stucked in, loud and wet.

I had several choices: I could step aside and let my man shoot the lieutenant. But the officer might be faster on the trigger and I was becoming very fond of Lambie. Or I could try for a distraction and go for my Luger.

While I was debating a rat as big as a house cat, flushed out of hiding by the lantern, scuffed across the cell, over the lieutenant's boots. He saw the dark ugly shape from the corner of an eye, jumped away, and shot it. That took his gun off me long enough. Mine was in my hand. I fired through his eye. The lantern sailed into the air. I caught it with my free hand, burned my fingers on the hot globe, but set it down without breaking it. The lieutenant fell on his face, staining the green slime with red.

Lambie made a pleased sound. I was pleased too that my movement hadn't surprised him, causing him to contract his trigger finger. I gave Lambie a fist of thanks on his shoulder, then we looked to the doctor. Fleming squinted, not yet accustomed to light. He looked up bewildered.

"I don't understand," he quavered. "Colonel Jerome asked me to return to lead the government. Why have I been arrested? Why were you brought here? Why are you so friendly with this soldier?"

"Later," I told him. "We'll talk about it."

Both David Hawk and Tara Sawyer had been emphatic about the doctor not discovering that we were involved in his being made president. I cursed them both. After Jerome's doublecross, I was tempted to tell the truth. But if they were right, if Fleming turned sulky and wouldn't play any more, who was going to keep the enemy off the island? So I lied my eyeballs off. If I could get Fleming to Noah, maybe the black patriarch could explain things to him.

I pointed to his foot. "How badly are you hurt?"

He still looked puzzled but I wanted him thinking of something other than politics.

He sighed. "My leg's broken."

I left Fleming to search the lieutenant's pockets for a key to the handcuff. It wasn't on him. I took the lantern to the chain and examined it. I could shoot the chain off, but I didn't have too much ammunition with me. I might need my bullets upstairs. A shot wasted here could make a difference in whether we made it away from the fort.

The mortar between the stones where the staple was anchored was a couple of centuries old, weakened by water seepage. I braced a foot against the wall and pulled. The chain was loose and moved a fraction of an inch, but it wouldn't come free. I tried a couple of times, but, it was no go. We'd have to dig it out.

I snapped my arm and the stiletto dropped out of
the chamois sheath into my curved fingers. The ra-
zor-sharp point bit into the mortar, chipped away a
pebble at a time. Lambie worked the staple. It took
more time than I liked. In spite of the cold, I was
sweating. If the lieutenant didn't show upstairs soon,
somebody would come looking, several somebodies.

I cut around one side of the staple. Then, with
both Lambie and me hauling on the chain, the tired
old metal broke. We stumbled back, slipping in the
oily slime. Fleming was yanked forward, but the
chain kept us from falling. When I caught my balance, I stuffed the loose end of the chain in the doctor's pocket and Lambie and I lifted him to his good
foot. He was wobbly from the ordeal. I left Lambie
to support him while I stripped off the lieutenant's
gold-braided coat. I also took the dead man's belt and
gun, handed them to Lambie and held the Doctor's
arm.

I told Lambie, "Get out of that jacket and into
this. You're being commissioned in the field."

Lambie complied. Carrying Fleming between us,
we went back to the guard room.

Mitzy Gardner's handsome chest heaved in relief.
She turned a chair for the doctor, saying as he sank
into it, "What kept you so long? We were just about
to come looking. God, what did they do to him?"

I snapped my fingers at Caco.

"Keys. Look in the drawers."

He opened the top drawer and tossed me a handful. I tried several before I found one that fit, then
the lock was so rusty I had to slam it with a paper

weight until it released. When the handcuff fell away, I saw the spikes inside and the drying blood around deep gashes on Fleming's wrist. Rust from the old handcuff was embedded in the cuts, but there was no way to wash them, no medication in the office. It would have to wait.

I explained my plan for leaving the fort. Lambie in his new uniform would stand with his back to the door. Caco was to tell the private on the drawbridge that the lieutenant wanted him inside. When he came, we would disarm him, then tie and gag him.

With the door cleared, Mitzy would go for the car, head it downhill close to the drawbridge while we brought Fleming across. He and I would curl up on the floor of the rear seat, Lambie in his braid would ride in the front between Mitzy and Caco.

At the sentry box Lambie would hold the lieutenant's gun on Mitzy, turned to face her. Caco would tell the corporal Jerome had ordered the girl brought to him. If it worked, fine. If it didn't, I had my Luger and Lambie and Caco were also armed. Three against three are very good odds.

We made it to the Caddy without trouble. Mitzy flipped on the headlights and drove downhill. The sentries saw us coming and moved out to the road, but not blocking it. They didn't expect a jailbreak. The corporal raised a hand to make a routine check and Mitzy stopped abreast of him. Caco leaned forward to screen Lambie from the soldiers and sounded disgusted.

"Colonel changed his mind. He wants the girl brought to him. Now."

The corporal looked worried. "Lieutenant, if you take her over yourself, who's in charge here?"

"You are," Lambie barked. "Don't pass anyone through until I come back. Drive on."

The corporal jumped back. Lambie's voice didn't match the real lieutenant's. "Hold on . . . you're not . . . What is this?"

I heard a gun explode and came to my knees. Caco had shot the corporal. The privates were caught off guard, but as Mitzy slammed the car ahead, one still grabbed at the door handle. I broke the hand with the snout of the Luger, then shot him. The other's rifle was whipping up when I put a bullet in his stomach. His rifle went off and plowed a hole in the door.

Then we were clear, swerving headlong down the drive. We were near the bottom when the Caddy sputtered and died. I knew the sound. We were out of gas. Mitzy coasted to a stop, looked around at me and shrugged. With the town under martial law, gas stations were closed. And Fleming was in no shape for a hike of more than twenty miles through the mountains.

We might carry him as far as Noah's hotel, but what then? He wouldn't be safe anywhere near Port of Spain when Jerome learned he was gone. We needed another car. We were still high enough so that I could see along the beach road. Out beyond the old town a jeep was parked. Dark figures passed nearby, in front of lanterns set across the highway, one of the colonel's roadblocks. I pointed it out to our group.

"There's our transportation. I don't know how

many we have to take it away from, and we can't risk gunfire to bring more troops swarming over us. You two wander down there, get them bunched while I cut around behind them. Mitzy, do you have a gun?"

The girl looked insulted. "Do I look undressed?"

"Stay here with the doctor. If anyone comes, shoot if you have to, but try a con first."

Lambie and Caco vanished along the dark road. I went down beyond the houses that faced the hill. The cottages were jammed against each other, with another row backed up to them. When there weren't any more houses, I was in jungle, the lanterns blinking farther ahead. Fern and green creepers cushioned any sound I might make. I flanked the jeep and eased out until I could see the patrol. I couldn't understand the words but whatever Lambie and Caco were saying must have been hilarious. The soldiers, four of them in a tight group, were doubled over, laughing, their backs toward me. I moved fast, before they turned, the Luger leveled. From close behind them, I said sharply, "There's a gun on all of you. Don't move."

The laughter stopped abruptly. They froze. Lambie backed away, raising his rifle, the gold braid shining in the lantern glow. Caco made a jump for the jeep, tilted into the back and came up with rope. The soldiers' heads followed him and I had a look at four astonished, frightened faces. Caco tied and gagged the soldiers. As he worked over the last one under Lambie's rifle, I checked the jeep for gas. It was a relief to find it full.

"Lose them back in the bush while I go for the doctor," I said. "And get the lanterns out of the road."

I drove the little vehicle back to the Caddy, wishing for a length of small hose to siphon fuel into the big car. And wishing for light. The headlights on the jeep didn't work. Mitzy had the rear door of the Cadillac open and Fleming on the edge of the seat ready to be moved. I picked him up and lifted him into the smaller car.

"Going to be a full load in this nutshell," I told the girl.

She climbed in beside me as I got behind the wheel again and said as I started downhill, "Lambie and Caco can ride the fenders as far as the hotel. Then they can get home by themselves."

It would have to be that way, but it wasn't good. Without headlights and without guidance, I couldn't follow the mountain road. The idea of trying to drive those winding curves in the dark made me shudder. I would have to run the gauntlet of the shore highway.

Lambie and Caco didn't want to be left behind, but finally gave in.

When they left, I started the jeep again. It was the first chance I'd had to ask Fleming more than the moment demanded. I called over my shoulder to him.

"Do you know what happened to Tara Sawyer? Did they let her leave?"

A groan answered. "No, they did not. The soldiers who took me to prison said she would be held for a million-dollar ransom. Where are you taking me?"

"To Noah."

Pain and anxiety filled his voice. "Yes, that first.

Then I must come down again. The people will listen
to me."

I let him kid himself. I had problems aplenty without arguments and explanations at this point. Not
the least of my troubles was Tara Sawyer. I couldn't
let anything happen to her.

I pushed the jeep, the throttle on the floor. The
quicker I delivered Fleming and Mitzy, the sooner I
could get back to town. I skidded a curve and saw
lanterns ahead. A second roadblock.

"Duck," I told Mitzy. "And hang tight."

I slowed. I wanted the men ahead to think we
would stop, to let me get close enough without arous-
ing their suspicions. Then I could gun through them
before they started shooting. After driving in the
dark, the lanterns blinded me. I was only thirty feet
from the soldiers when I saw it—a massive truck
sprouting a small, rapid fire howitzer at the rear. It
was parked crosswise and filled the whole road. I was
not going to gun through that.

On one side of us the oily waters of the swamp reflected the lanterns. I wouldn't get far that way. On
the other side were palm trees. Palms don't grow in
water so there would be solid ground, but the trees
were too close together for comfort, in a staggered
pattern up a slope. The jeep could jam between them.
But of the choices, this was the only one possible.

I whipped the wheel and kicked the accelerator,
bouncing off the road. I heard them yell for me to
halt, then a rifle fired. The bullet clicked through
palm leaves, high, a warning shot. Mitzy was twisted
in the seat, shooting back. I didn't look. I was dodg-

ing trees, dancing that jeep like a Virginia Reel. I
sideswiped one tree, bounched off with two wheels
off the ground, nearly tipping over. Then the car
dropped back and I slammed through a gap, grinding
metal on all four fenders. Guns tracked us by sound,
but the soldiers couldn't see us. Beyond the truck I
fought back to the road and found another surprise.

They had a jeep there and four men running to it.
I cut in just past it with a glimpse of the army piling
in. Loud gasps of pain came from Fleming. It was a
rough ride until we leveled out. Mitzy fired over
Fleming while I got as much speed as possible out of
the little car. It wasn't going to be enough. One of
our tires had blown.

Mitzy yelled, "Nick, they're coming up on us."

She didn't need to tell me. Their bullets stung past
us almost as soon as I heard the shots. I passed her
the Luger.

"Try for a tire. Draw a line across it and keep
pumping lead."

She used both hands, but shooting at a moving target from a moving station doesn't allow much aiming. This was one of those times when I wondered if
my name was about to be added to the list Hawk
keeps in his safe, a star beside each line to signify
deceased.

Mitzy yelped. I thought she was hit, but she had
sat back on her knees, straight up. In the rear-view
mirror I saw why. I was just in time to catch the car
behind us go into a drunken swerve at full speed. It
spun and went tail down in the swamp. As it sank,
marsh gas boiled up around it in bursting bubbles.

The headlights glittered on just before they blanked out.

Mitzy put the Luger on the seat then squared around. We limped ahead on the broken tire. It wasn't the only sound in the night. Off in the jungle there was a rattle of bamboo rods beating against a log drum.

It was a dim sound, eerie in that it seemed to fill the air as light fills it and is part of it. I wondered if Caco and Lambie were getting out a wireless message to the tribe, or whether it was a progress report on us, sent ahead by dark figures invisible in the jungle forest.

The tempo quickened. I sensed an urgency. From the back seat Dr. Fleming spoke, his voice weak with pain.

"We are being followed, and they're coming on fast."

I leaned on the jeep, wheedling the last jet of speed it had left.

SIX

Ahead on the road a torch was being held high, waving us to a turn. I didn't stop to ask questions. I took the angle. I fought the car through the sand toward another torch down at the shoreline, skidded to a stop and cut the engine.

Noah was there, tall, scrawny without his white robe, wearing only a narrow cloth around his groin. In the silence, as the motor died, I heard a full-throttled roar on the highway. We were out of time. Out of running room. Our back was to the sea. And my Luger was empty. I didn't think the stiletto was a match for the rifles bearing down on us. Mitzy was already out of the jeep, kicking off her sandals, beckoning to me. Noah bent into the back, scooped Fleming into his long arms, and lifted him out.

Noah said calmly, "Come along, Carter. Take Mitzy's hand, don't let go. Keep behind me."

I shoved the Luger under my belt, took the girl's hand and followed. Noah walked into the water.

What was to argue? There wasn't an alternative left that I knew of. We were going to be dead in a short time anyway. And maybe, if we could swim far enough before our pursuers hit the beach, our heads wouldn't be seen if we kept them low enough in the dark swells.

The bottom sand gave under my feet, slurring away. Noah moved deliberately, cradling Fleming against his chest with ease. The sea surface rose around the big man's legs, halfway up his thighs, then he began rising in short lurches, a foot at a time. Behind him Mitzy Gardner sank to her breasts. Then she began to rise too.

With my next step my toe stubbed against rock. I stumbled, almost pitched down, then raised my foot, scraping it against the stone while the two people ahead of me stopped, waiting while I caught my balance. I moved my foot forward and found a step, put my weight on it, straightened my knee and felt a second step above the first. We climbed four of them, then leveled off, walking on a rough, flat top of something six inches below the water.

I had a belly laugh. This kind of magic I understood. This was the straight path on which I'd watched Noah come to us the first time. Now I realized there was some old structure here, probably an ancient breakwater that had sunk in an earthquake long before the memory of the present inhabitants. I didn't think Noah was old enough to have seen it above water. He had probably discovered it accidentally, swimming, and wily old showman that he was, had made capital of it to spook his superstitious tribe.

Ahead of me Mitzy giggled. "You're being honored, Nick. Let in on the secret nobody else knows. Just watch for slippery spots and don't wander. The top is only two feet wide."

I squeezed her hand hard enough to hurt. She had it coming.

"You knew it and tried to snow me, ratfink. How did you find out about it?"

"Swimming. I butted my head against it good, knocking myself out. I was half-drowned when Noah hauled me ashore. He didn't tell me what I'd hit until I said I was going to find out anyway, then he made me promise not to blow it to anyone else."

We were almost at the headland when two light beams swept across the water and shouts came to us, angry and frustrated. The jeep had been found but the prey was gone. We were beyond the reach of the beams and couldn't be seen.

The breakwater ended against a sheer limestone cliff. A flight of steps had been cut out of the wall. Narrow. Only one person at a time could go up. The builders of that fortress had sat up there and thumbed their noses at the king's ships when they tried to penetrate the cove.

It was a long climb but Noah was not winded when he took us past the top step and dropped five feet to the flat platform that did double duty as footing for defenders and roof for the lower rooms. I thought he ought to be teaching AXE's physical fitness course. He handed Fleming down to reaching arms and the doctor was hurried into a room.

When we followed, I saw it was already prepared for him. Torches burned in brackets around the stone walls. A thick pallet of aromatic leaves was waiting in the center of the floor. We had walked through an aisle of silent tribesmen, people who reached to touch the doctor lightly as though offering him their strength.

As Fleming was lowered onto the pallet, I said, "He has a broken leg and a wrist full of rust. There'll be blood poisoning and I didn't have time to stop by the corner drugstore. He needs antibiotics right away. Any chance of having them brought up here?"

The tall black man moved his head sideways, unconcerned as far as I could tell. Fleming sounded weaker but he was smiling.

"Thank you for your concern, Mr. Carter, but I am in the best possible hands. I'll trust Noah's medical know-how over the biggest Park Avenue specialist."

The patriarch said softly, "We had word of the injuries in advance and are prepared."

He indicated a row of bowls beside the pallet. They held liquids and bandaging cloths. Two women pull off Fleming's clothes leaving only his shorts, then Noah knelt by him, dipped a sponge in the liquids, washed the rust out of Fleming's wrist and plastered it with a greenish mess.

"This is a hot poultice of cochan leaves cooked with yellow soap," Noah said to me. "We bind it on so, with cloth. It will draw the poison and the arm will soon heal."

For the broken leg the treatment was more intricate. Noah set the bone, laid out splints, dipped a finger in a bowl of dark red cream-thick substance, drew a circle over the break, made an "X" inside it, and smiled at me.

"Cock's blood," he said, "to absorb the devil from

the leg. Now a thick coat of sureau and barrachin leaves, over that a cast of hot corn meal and a tight bandage."

On top of it all he bound the splints. How much of the act was old tribal herb medicine, proven effective through ages of trial, how much was psychological faith healing, I didn't know. But Fleming was their boy, one of them, and if he really believed in this mixture of native cures and sorcery, maybe he would come through. Like many highly educated men of all races, I suspected he nursed a hard core of religiousness. And I also suspected that though he might not profess it in public, his heart accepted the banned mystique of voodoo. But I couldn't stay here to see how it all went.

I drew Noah aside and asked, "Did the drums tell you Fleming wants to go back and make speeches?"

"They told me." The tall man's smile was twisted. "The doctor is an idealist and stubborn in his beliefs. But after he is out of shock, I will make him understand the truth. You, I assume, are returning for Miss Sawyer?"

I had not said so, hadn't mentioned the hotel tycoon's daughter. He appeared to know one whale of a lot for somebody isolated on top of this hill. It could be the drums that kept him alerted, of course, combined with a very sophisticated power of reasoning that gave meaning to the scraps of information coming through the jungle.

My face felt a little stiff as I said, "If I don't bring her out in one piece, I won't be in one piece myself for long."

Mitzy had listened in. Now she said, "You're nuts to try that, but if you do, I'm going along. Us girls ought to stick together."

"Wrong guess," I said. "You're a distraction I can't afford. Noah, keep her here."

He surprised me by nodding. "I'll send a guide down the trail with you. . . ."

"No dice," I cut in. "The jeep's way up at the cove, it'll take too long that way. I'll go the way we came."

He raised his eyebrows high, not arguing. He knew he couldn't change my mind. With a lift to his shoulders, he took Mitzy's arm and went back to Fleming.

I headed down the steps, leaving behind me a rising chant from the tribe. I supposed it was a call to the gods to speed the Doctor's healing. At the bottom I stepped on the breakwater, took a bearing on the jeep I could barely make out as a dark blob against the lighter sand, and went straight toward it. The car seemed to be alone; the soldiers were gone.

Concentrating on direction, I was halfway across when my foot came down on a slimy patch of sea grass growing in the rock and I skidded off, over my head. I came up sputtering, climbed on top again, lined up once more with the headland and the jeep, and went on more carefully. I got wet again where the breakwater ended, then I was ashore, soaked through.

Stripping, I wrung out my skirt, dried the Luger as much as the damp cloth would allow me to, dried the bullets in my ammo belt and dropped them on the front seat. The clothes I spread on the hood where the heat from the engine would dry them after a couple of miles. I kept my boots on. They squashed as I walked, but I needed them for driving.

I figured I'd have a drunken ride on the wobbling flat tire and wasn't disappointed. As I neared the site where the other jeep had gone down in the swamp, I braked and loaded the Luger. There was activity at the spot, three or four figures standing at the edge of the road. I figured the men who had been in the car had escaped drowning, but I couldn't see what they were doing.

One of them stepped into the middle of the road, waving me on. I almost shot him before I saw the loincloth and knew he and the others were not soldiers. I kept hold of the gun anyway, leveled, easing forward. I heard laughter, a grunting chant, then from the dark swamp the nose of the jeep surfaced like some dripping monster. They had a line on it, lifting it clear, throwing another line to pull it sideways onto the edge of the road. It was empty, no soldiers in it.

Noah's little jungle helpers were taking the wheel off the axle, rolling it toward me. Here was my fresh tire with air in it. I climbed down and watched while two of them picked up the nose of my jeep, changed the wheels and set it down with wide grins that told me all was well again. Then they disappeared into the palm trees. If I had blinked, I'd have missed seeing it, the way they melted among the palms.

I rolled on fast, wondering what I'd find further on, where the big truck had blocked the road. Noah's people were working there too, but the truck was too heavy for their vine ropes and wouldn't budge. I got down, shoved through them, climbed behind the wheel and started the motor. I waved them out of the way and threw the truck into reverse, then jumped to the ground. It backed into the swamp, sinking out of sight except for the last foot of the long gun. The men were gone when I looked away from the bubbling gas.

I saw nobody else between there and the old resort hotel. In the kitchen a couple of men were gambling. The game was new to me. Each man had a polished bone shaped remarkably like a human finger. Taking turns they rolled their bones across the table. Whichever stopped closest to the center crack won the round, to judge by the excitement. Caco was the last to try his luck and when his joint landed in the crack itself he made a low, happy shout. The losers paid him double.

He and Lambie dropped out of the game to listen to me explain our next target. When I said I wanted them to take me inside the Sawyer hotel, they were notably unenthusiastic.

Lambie coughed apologetically. "It's one thing to have trapped the lieutenant at the fort," he said, "But fool the colonel? I don't think so."

I needed these two, needed them willing and confident for a delicate operation, not nervous and doubtful.

"Noah knows where we're going," I told them. "And he'll help."

That did it. If Noah thought it was all right, it

was going to be all right. We went out to the jeep in
high spirits.

The downtown streets were still empty, only about
a half dozen people out. When they heard the jeep,
they ducked inside like mice. There was no traffic
and all the buildings were closed up, their windows
blank—all except the lower floor of the Sawyer
Grand LaClare hotel. I drove into the crescent drive
with Caco's rifle against the back of my neck and
"Lieutenant" Lambie sitting beside him, a short gun
in his lap. We stopped in the rectangle of light before
the open front entrance. A sentry in the shadow beside the door watched us. Lambie got out and leveled
his gun on me while Caco dropped out on his side,
stepped away and ordered me to the ground with a
jerk of his muzzle. With a soldier on either side, we
marched forward. The sentry blocked our way.

"Sorry, sir. Colonel says nobody goes in tonight."

Lambie drew himself up with military ferocity.
"We go in or you'll be stood against the wall. This
prisoner is the Nick Carter Jerome will give a thousand dollars for. Stand aside."

"Oh." The sentry swung his rifle on me and licked
his lips. "In that case I'll take him in, sir."

Lambie roared. "Oh, no, you won't. I deliver him
myself. Don't think you can grab off that reward.
Move."

The sentry looked guilty and didn't move fast
enough. Caco stepped past me and lashed his gun
barrel against the man's ear, knocking him down.
Caco's finger snapped against his trigger. The shot
went between my legs, too high for comfort. The ac-

© Lorillard 1975

C'mon

Come for the filter.   ## You'll stay for the taste.

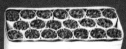

KENT

WITH THE FAMOUS MICRONITE FILTER

KING SIZE

© Lorillard 1975

Newport

Alive with pleasure!

20 CLASS A CIGARETTES

Newport

Newport

MENTHOL KINGS

7 mg. "tar", 1.2 mg. nicotine, av. per cigarette, FTC Report Apr. '75.

Warning: The Surgeon General Has Determined That Cigarette Smoking Is Dangerous to Your Health.

tion was getting a little too real. Lambie roared again.

"The colonel. Where is he?"

A very frightened sentry scuttled on his butt against the wall, stammering, "Yes, sir, in the casino, sir. Shall I show you, sir?"

"I believe we can find it ourselves." Lambie's voice was a dry threat. "Stay at your post."

Caco prodded me past and into the lobby. Thomas Sawyer would go through the roof to see it now, a wreck. The big sofas were slashed, spilling stuffing and springs, newsstands were overturned, papers and magazines torn and trampled on the floor, trinkets and candies were looted. The glass fronts of the shops were broken in, racks and shelves emptied, walls stripped of the exotic baubles, "native" mats and masks manufactured by the ton in the cheap labor ports of the world. What a mess! Colonel Carib Jerome might be a class conspirator, but he was one hell of a lousy commander to let his army take the place apart. He could've made a bundle out of it later, after he won his game.

The casino looked worse than the lobby. Gambling tables that cost in the thousands were knocked over, broken. Roulette wheels were smashed so their rigging and magnets spilled among the tumbled chips. The painting of cavorting nudes above the long bar was carved up, the figures cut out like paper dolls. Caco and Lambie whistled.

"Some jump-up we missed."

Under the painting the rows on rows of glasses had been swept to the floor. A few empty liquor bottles lay shattered against the front of the bar. The rest were gone. I mentioned that.

"Jerome's liberation army has got itself liberally loaded."

My men looked around the cavernous, empty rooms uneasily. "Where'd they all go? Where's the colonel?"

"In bed. Where else, with three hundred rooms here? Except for Jerome. I bet he's tucked himself away in Chip Cappola's office to count the loot from the tables. Let's go visit him."

We went on to the cashiers' booths. These alone were unviolated, pristine; there were no stacks of coins behind the glass partition, no trays, no bills in the open drawers. The soldiers had been kept away from here and the temptation of the till. I borrowed a knee from Caco to step up on the counter, bent over the glass partition and unlatched the door to the inside hall. The boys walked me through.

Jeb, the burly black guard, was still at his bank of control switches. Maybe he had changed sides, but it was more likely he was Jerome's man to begin with, with eyes and ears trained to report on the hotel. We surprised him. He made a grab for the gun in his desk, saw Caco's rifle in my spine, recognized me and laughed.

"Upon my word, Mr. Carter. Where'd you find him, Lieutenant?"

Lambie swaggered, waving his gun airily. "Picked him up at a roadblock. Tell the colonel we're here."

Jeb lifted a finger. He wasn't ready to announce us. "Miss Mitzy left here with Carter. Where's she?"

Lambie shrugged eloquently. "Wasn't anyone with him tonight. Maybe she cleared out with the mob."

"Well, she don't count." Jeb stabbed the intercom to Cappola's office and purred into it. "Colonel, you have guests."

Annoyment rattled back. "I said nobody. . . . ."

"Mr. Nick Carter and two soldiers bringing him."

The voice from the office changed to a bark of satisfaction. "That's different. Send them along."

Jeb buzzed the office door, it slid back and we went in. Carib Jerome was at Cappola's desk, bundles of paper currency and trays of coin filling the top of it, more of the same stacked on the floor. All the operating cash of the casino, plus the day's receipts from the hotel and the shops around the lobby, was here —one hell of a lot of Syndicate and Sawyer money. The colonel had a computer to count it. I smiled at him.

"Found a system to beat the wheels, Jerome?"

He returned the smile, but it was chillier than mine. "The very best, you must admit." He looked beyond me at Lambie. "Lieutenant, where is the girl who was with this man?"

I threw it out flat. "Dead. Drowned."

The black eyes narrowed and the ebony head moved slowly, side to side, the voice gliding from lips that barely moved.

"She swims like a dolphin, Mr. Carter. Do not try to deceive me. She is a valuable property in Miami."

I glanced over my shoulder at the door, still open, Jeb an interested audience in the hall. With him behind my men, I couldn't pull the Luger on Jerome.

I'd get Caco and Lambie shot. I wanted that door closed and the quickest way was to make the colonel wary of the guard.

I told Jerome, "You might get a ransom for Mitzy, but I bet this lieutenant never sees his reward for me from your sticky fingers."

The door slid shut on Jeb. Jerome dropped his eyes on the table, reaching for a packet of bills. When he held it forward and raised his head, he looked down the barrel of the Luger.

"Take what you want, help yourselves," I told Caco and Lambie. Then, as Jerome's hand edged toward the intercom to call Jeb, I said, "No, colonel. Roll the chair back."

He didn't move, but his hand dropped to his side. He looked from Lambie to Caco as their guns veered from me to him and his face tightened.

"Treachery, Mr. Carter? Bribing soldiers? They'll be courtmartialed as soon as I. . . ."

He was fast. I knew he would be. Dropping behind the desk, he swept his fingers toward his holster. I was a little faster, swapping the Luger to my other hand, snapping out the stiletto, flipping it. It pinned his cuff against the holster and spoiled his draw.

He wasn't chicken, I gave him that. He'd taken a big risk and if he'd gotten a shot in, the noise would've brought Jeb with a shotgun. But he hadn't and he knew when to stop. For the moment anyway. He straightened in the chair, his hands loose, and relaxed to wait for another chance. I cocked the Luger and told him to lean against the wall so we could see what he had on him.

His eyes fired hate at me but he stood up, carefully, and assumed the position. Lambie laid his short gun on a pile of bills and went over the colonel, from neck to boots. He tossed me my knife, the holstered gun, and found a little holdout in a pocket that he dropped in one of mine.

"Now, sit down on the couch and be comfortable so we can talk. Where's Tara Sawyer?" I said.

Jerome didn't bat an eye. He sat back, one arm over the top of the couch, and crossed his legs. He curled his lip and said in an easy voice. "Where is Mitzy Gardner?"

I didn't have time for question-and-answer games, nor to search the whole hotel, for it was logical he would keep Tara here. I couldn't be sure Jerome's entire army was in drunken sleep upstairs, so I could be trapped searching for my girl. I stood over the colonel and raked the front sight of the Luger down his cheek. It left a bleeding gash and made him wince. I didn't want to kill him; he was the only man who could control the military, and I'd still need him and them. But before I went into that, I wanted to be sure of Tara's safety.

I told Jerome that, adding, "But I don't mind spoiling your face if I have to."

He was a handsome man, knew it, and was vain of it. "Very well," he said. "I doubt you could take her anyway. Miss Sawyer is in her suite on the top floor. There are 600 men between here and there."

SEVEN

While Lambie covered the colonel, Caco and I took off Jerome's jacket and shirt, tore the shirt into strips to tie him and gag him with, and left him on the couch.

"You stay and keep an eye on Jerome," I told Caco, showing him the remote control for the door. "Wait for Lambie and me to get there, crack it open enough for us to go through, then close it. We'll put the guard out of action and go for the girl."

Lambie shoved his gun in my back again and we went out. Jeb was studying a racing form and didn't look up. I had the Luger at my side out of his sight. When I was close enough, I shoved it up under Jeb's nose. While he gaped at it, Lambie used his gun butt on the round head, hard. Jeb fell against the desk, then rolled to the floor. Whether or not he was dead depended on how thick his skull was. If he did wake up, I didn't want him opening the office door so we used his shirt to truss him, dragged him to the cashier's cage and tied him to the stool there so he couldn't crawl. Then Lambie and I crossed the wrecked casino, heading for the elevators.

We were halfway across the lobby when an elevator door opened, a soldier staggered out, saw our guns and tried to duck back. I threw the stiletto, caught him in the jugular, dropping him without sound. Lambie hauled him behind the registration desk. There were no keys to Tara's suite in the mail box, no keys in any of them, so I'd have to break in and not make any noises. We went back to the elevator and I collected the two gilded machetes the soldier had looted off the wall and dropped when he died.

So far so good. Now there were only 599 military guards to watch out for in the hotel. Of course, heaven only knew how many more were outside. We rode the elevator cage to the top, and ran for Tara's door. I picked the lock with the stiletto and we were inside before anyone showed up in the hall.

The room was stifling, the air-conditioning turned off. Tara Sawyer lay spreadeagle on the bed in panties and bra. The underwear was not all she wore. There was tape, a lot of it, around her wrists and ankles and secured under the bed frame so she couldn't move. But she wasn't gagged. The sound-proofing of the Sawyer Grand LaClare made that unnecessary. She could have yelled her head off and no one but the men in the next room would hear her.

She saw me and Lambie. Her face contorted with despair and her mouth opened to scream. I jumped and clapped a hand over her lips, speaking in a whisper.

"Jerome's men are here. Be quiet."

Her eyes flicked to Lambie. She thought I was a captive too. I told her he was on our side. The blue eyes went wide, dark, deep with anger rather than fear. I took the hand off her mouth and covered her lips with mine. I let her go to cut the tapes away while she whispered a question about Dr. Fleming. Had they killed him?

"No," I said. "We got him away. He's hurt, but safe up in the mountains with Noah."

"Who?"

Of course, she'd probably never heard of the old black giant or his tribe . . . or his bag of tricks.

"You'd call me a liar if I tried to tell you about Noah, but if we get out of this town alive, I'll show you. Even then you won't believe it."

I pulled the tape off quickly, to keep the pain as short as possible. Fresh perspiration sprang on her forehead in large individual drops. Her hands and feet were discolored, purpling and swollen because the tape had been too tight. She was in agony as the blood began flowing again, biting her lips, tears starting in her eyes. She couldn't stand and it would be some time before she could walk. Still, I couldn't risk carrying her through the hotel. If anyone tried to stop us, I'd need my hands and maybe Lambie's too.

I wrapped Tara's ankles and wrists in cold wet towels from the bathroom, letting them soak in. Then brought a cotton dress from the closet, helped her to sit up and put it over her head. She looked better without the dress, but the skimpy panties and bra weren't exactly suitable as a travelling costume.

It took precious minutes before Tara could put weight on her feet, and more time passed while I walked her around the room until she could move on her own. Then I sent Lambie into the hall to make sure it was clear. When he put his head back through the door and nodded, Tara and I followed him in a hurry to the elevator. We ducked into the cage, and I pushed the lobby button just as a room door opened down the corridor.

We dropped to the floor and the elevator door began to slide. Through a crack I saw soldiers. Worse, I saw Colonel Carib Jerome, with a pistol leveled on the crack.

I dodged behind the metal door and hit the basement button as he fired. The lead slammed into the rear of the cage and ricocheted. It had to be magic that it hit none of us. Then the door closed and we went down. It took an hour by my count and we had to be mere minutes. I knew Jerome and company would be on our heels in the other car. If there was no transportation in the garage or if the ramp was blocked, David Hawk would be out of one more operative. Tom Sawyer would lose his daughter and Noah, bless his faking heart, would lose one hell of a good man.

Where Noah's other man was, I didn't ask myself. Probably dead. If Jerome had snowed Caco into letting him out of the office with a bribe, Caco had a bullet coming. The colonel was resourceful. It was obviously a mistake to have left poor, simple Caco alone with such a sharpie.

The elevator cage squashed on the air buffer at the basement floor, and we were in the garage. There were lots of cars here, appropriated from the evacuated guests and staff, but I didn't expect keys in them and I couldn't spare a second to look. A military truck was parked at the bottom of the ramp; it would probably be ready to move on short notice. But it looked to be a mile away. I pointed at it.

"You two make a run for that," I said. "Get it started while I keep the elevator bottled up."

They sprinted, Lambie holding Tara's arm, the girl still not sure-footed but game to make the try. I saw them start, then faced the elevator. The indicator needle moved, tracking the descent, then stopped. The door began sliding open in front of me.

When it was two inches apart I poured lead in, heard a scream and hoped it was Jerome. I kept firing as the crack widened and there were more cries until somebody had the wit to start the car back up. I shot until the door closed, then ran for the truck. Lambie was in the back under the canvas top. Tara had the engine roaring and had left the driver's seat for me. I thanked her for that. If it had been Mitzy Gardner, I'd have had an argument and there just wasn't time. As it was, I still didn't know what I'd run into outside.

I got under the wheel and gunned up the ramp in second gear. There was no barricade at the top. I headed for the road. At the front of the hotel I took a quick look and saw Jerome and soldiers erupting from the door. They stopped on the top step to throw rifle fire after us, but they hurried too much. The shots went low.

I careened from side to side to further spoil their aim and heard Lambie blasting with his short gun from the rear. I yelled at him to lie low behind the tailgate, but either he didn't hear me or was too keyed-up to think. Then it was too late. I heard a short scream. In the rear-view mirror I saw Lambie stagger and pitch out of the jeep. He was lying very still in the middle of the drive.

The whole front of his shirt was soaked in blood. More bullets riddled his body, as if Jerome was making Lambie die for those of us he couldn't reach. A shot exploded into Lambie's head, taking half of it away. I concentrated on my driving; it took away some of the sickness at the pit of my belly.

The firing stopped. The mirror showed Jerome and his troops running for cars parked around the hotel entrance. We were still a long way from home. At the boulevard I skidded the rear wheels for the turn, straightened out and tramped the gas pedal against the floor. The truck was powered to carry heavy loads but not built for racing. We had a head start, but not enough to outrun the colonel.

We were past the shuttered city, bearing on Noah's hotel, with decisions to make. I couldn't beat Jerome on the shore highway. The choice was between hiding the truck in the old hotel's shed and holing up inside or tackling the goat trail over the mountains. I thought the colonel probably knew about Noah's use of the place and could trap us there. He wouldn't even need to risk a fight. The building was tinder. He could burn it around us.

So it was the mountain trail. Our heavy truck could probably grind through the potholes with less damage than the lighter cars behind us, and they couldn't cover the ground any faster than I.

Their headlights hadn't picked us up by the time

we hit the turn. I cut our lights, threw the wheel over, and was out of sight in the jungle growth when two jeeps clattered past on the highway. That was just fine with me. I stopped, took the flashlight out of its bracket, and went around to investigate the back of the truck. Maybe Lambie had dropped his gun inside. My ammo was running low.

There was no gun among the clutter of rope, shovels, excavation equipment, and three crates. As I turned away, the light beam fell on a stenciled word on a box. "Dyamite." With a hand on the tailgate, I swung over it. The box was open and some of the sticks were gone, but most of them were still bedded in the sawdust packing.

Colonel Jerome wouldn't go far on the highway when he saw I was not ahead of him. He would be back. And now I could be ready for him. We were a hundred yards into the jungle track. I dropped out of the truck, worked as I ran back toward the intersection, and had a charge put together by the time Jerome's jeeps showed up. They came fast, made the turn, their lights sweeping over me where I crouched in the brush. Then they discovered the dark truck and bumped toward it with triumphant yells. As the lead car came on, I lit the fuse. When it went by, I threw the stick in the rear seat and dropped flat, burying my nose in the vines.

The explosion was immediate and close. The shock wave picked me up and threw me back in the road, stunned but in better condition than the men who'd been in the car. I lay dragging breath, hearing Tara's voice and the sound of her feet as she came running toward me. I got up before I wanted to, waving her back, seeing the deep crater blown out of the road. Behind me a second jeep was nearing the turn. The girl and I made it to our truck, were in gear and moving when the jeep jammed to a stop at the crater. The rear-view mirror showed me Jerome's tall figure scrambling to the ground, standing in the lights. Lead reached for us, fell short, and we pulled away.

Tara was all questions. I explained my find, bent to kiss her briefly while I fought the road.

"We're all right now," I told her. "They can't come past that hole unless they cut some trees, and that'll take awhile. Just set yourself for a roller-coaster ride."

In the dark I almost rammed a tree at a turn. That made me realize we needed light to drive by and I switched them on. My watch showed me the night was waning. By the time we reached the roughest spots, there should be enough dawn to help. Under the roof of leaves where we were now there was only blackness, my headlights tunneling through. We ground ahead, Tara hanging onto the door to keep from being tossed against the top of the cab. She took it in silence for some miles, then gave me an apologetic laugh.

"Nick, I do believe I'm not cut out for this. I came on like gangbusters at the idea of coming here to help Dr. Fleming. It seemed very romantic." Her laugh was embarrassed. "Now I see what it's really like."

"You learn if you're in it." I grinned at her.

So she was scared, talking to build herself up. We were coming to the top and she was going to be more scared. It gave me a very good excuse for relaxing both of us. I cut the motor. It was very quiet. I got down, opened Tara's door and pulled her out. I led her into the bright beam ahead of the truck where I could see that we wouldn't bed down on a snake or a porcupine. I took her in my arms.

Fright can be a very good aphrodisiac. Her mouth was as hungry as mine. Her body moved under my hands in a long undulating caress.

It was a long time before we collapsed, spent. But we couldn't stay here. We stood up and I kissed her forehead. In the truck again, I smiled. "Feel better?"

She nodded, lying back relaxed with her eyes closed. Because of stopover in the forest there was plenty of light when we reached the precipice. I told Tara to keep her eyes closed for the next half mile. Of course, she opened them immediately, looked over the edge, and some of my good work was spoiled. She sat rigid, pale, but with her head high, chin up. Tara Sawyer was O.K. in my book.

We scraped along the cliff, gears whining, and then were past the danger point, on the last long lap of the footpath. My thoughts switched to Dr. Fleming.

We lurched up to where the road petered out, left the truck and climbed. I discovered something I hadn't noticed on the trek down. The path went up one side of a steep ravine; behind the edge, on the far side, were caves where the overflow of the tribe made its homes. No one appeared to be in at the moment.

The thick plank gate of the fortress was closed. It didn't budge when I shoved and I used the butt of the Luger on it, yelling for Noah to let us in. It was a few minutes before I heard chains clank and timber lifted out of sockets. Then the gate swung inward and the man in the white robe waved us through.

Tara looked at the long frame open-mouthed; he backed so the gate could be closed and barred again.

Noah welcomed the girl with gentle courtesy, told us Dr. Fleming was improving, then went on to the bad news.

"Our communication line went silent last night so we have had no word from the lowlands since you left. Can you tell me how the situation is developing in Port of Spain?"

Obviously, that the old resort hotel at the edge of town was more than simple camping grounds for the tribe's visits to town. It had to be a nerve center for reports gathered in the capital, the starting point for the messages that had been relayed to the drums. If there had been no recent messages, that meant Jerome had raided the place.

Tiredness washed through me. I'd been on the move too long. This old fortress had been impregnable against kings, ships and ancient scaling parties from the sea. But today we only had my Luger and a handful of ammunition, Mitzy Gardner's little gun, and a few cases of dynamite. Not much against a modern army. My guts quaked with weariness and I leaned against a corner of the thick rock wall to sketch in the picture for the old man. I finished by telling about my plans for the dynamite.

"I should've blown that cliff while I was there," I confessed. "But I didn't think of it then and it's too far away to do it now. Jerome will be up that way with jeeps sometime today. I want to mine that trail, and I'll need porters."

Noah picked out a labor crew while I introduced the girls. Mitzy took Tara in tow to find her a place to sleep.

EIGHT

The porters carried the dynamite from the truck. They took the open half box into the fortress and left one full crate for planting above the shore road. Before I left the truck, I took the rotor out of the distributor so no one else could start it.

I mined the trail with dynamite, rigging fuses so a single man could explode each charge independent of the others. While I worked, I heard drums within the fortress; these were not messages but deep-throated ceremonial sounds. Noah, I suspected, was drumming up courage in his entourage.

It was broad daylight by the time I finished. I was out of steam and starved when I dragged in through the gate. There was indeed a ritual in full swing. The sacrificial fowls were already killed and boiling in a pot. Dancers were circling it with spears and painted shields. They had great gear to face a bazooka with. Noah came out, saw me and sent women to tug me to a drumhead table. They sat me on a stump of pulpy wood and brought food, half an avacado stuffed with wild papaya and shredded pineapple soaked in lime juice, a gourd of shellfish, a cocoanut filled with white rum, sugar syrup and more lime. It was subtle going down, but in my depleted condition the mixture would knock me out soon.

111

Trying to stay awake long enough to finish eating, I concentrated on what I was supposed to be doing here. My job was to put Fleming in the presidential chair and keep him there unharmed. There was no doubt of his popularity with the people, he could win an election hands down. But most of them had no arms or military training. They might be willing to fight for him, but they were no match for Colonel Carib Jerome and his professionals. And Russia's Big Brother stance didn't help.

I don't know when I blanked out. Next thing I knew Noah was shaking me awake. I lay in a cool, dim room; the shadow line at the door put the sun at mid-afternoon. I had left a man on the trail as a spotter. He would hear approaching cars a long distance off, with plenty of time to warn us. He was here behind Noah now, excited.

When I sat up, the old man said, "The army has reached the truck."

I was wide awake now. "How many?"

"He can't count," Noah spoke for the spotter. He says "Many. Many."

I got up and trotted to the gate. They must have started up the trail by now and I wanted to be sure they hadn't discovered or evaded the dynamite. The war dance was over and people who had gone to their caves were hurrying back to the fort.

Passing Dr. Fleming's room I hauled up short. He stood in front of the door between the two girls, on one foot, the splintered leg bent back in a hammock. There were no angry red streaks snaking up his bandaged arm, no gray under the rich chocolate of his face. There wasn't time to look into it further now, but Fleming's recovery amazed me. I put it out of mind and went on, listening for sounds as I turned down the path. If they were advancing fast enough, I might walk into them.

I hadn't heard a thing by the time I reached the fuses. This was in a natural clearing and over the trees I could see the truck at the bottom of the ravine a quarter of a mile below. The thirty or so men lounging around the truck had not yet started up. I wondered why. Then I heard a sound behind me and Mitzy was there with the explanation. Just what I needed.

"There's another attack, Nick. Boats are coming into the cove, a lot of them."

That at least answered why the bunch below wasn't on its way. It was a pincer move, radio-controlled to start on the fortress from two directions at the same time. I put an arm around the girl's shoulder.

"Can you obey orders?"

"It's been my life's work. What do you want me to do?"

I pulled her down to the ground, showed her the fuses, and gave her my lighter, explaining what to do.

"The path is mined between those two points." I pointed to them. "The fuse on the right will blow the lowest charge three minutes after it's lit. The progression moves to the left, with the charges twenty feet apart. When the advance group reaches the turn, start the first burn. I hope that's all you'll need but some soldiers are pigheaded. Take your time setting them off. But stop them."

"A bloody pleasure." She gave me her lips and I got the notion she was saying goodbye. "Good luck with the armada."

I grinned. "We'll make it. Just keep the faith with Noah."

I sounded far better than I felt. We were not equipped to stand off a prolonged siege on two fronts. I would do what I could with the realities, but my bones told me it would take a miracle for any of us to survive the day.

I got back to the gate as fast as I could. The scene inside had changed in the short while I'd been away. The tribe was busy. A bucket line passed stones the size of a skull from a stockpile and up the ladders set against the low continuous roof. Other bucket lines led into rooms at the two outer corners of the fortress. They were setting up concentrations of firepower at those points.

There was a fever of excitement about the rhythmic side-to-side swaying of black arms, receiving and passing material on. And, oddly, there was also an air of absolute confidence in these men and women who had never in their lives fought a flesh-and-blood army.

Noah himself while still serene, seemed less secure than his people. He was arguing with Dr. Fleming in an island of quiet near the gate, away from the activity. Fleming leaned on a crutch, sputtering, insisting.

"Very well, Noah, I accept Jerome's duplicity. But I cannot permit you and your people to throw your

lives away on my account. If Jerome is so power
hungry, I must submit as I did to Hammond. I will
surrender, allow myself to be exiled to the United
States. Jerome is a competent man and this island
has survived under military rule before. Perhaps I
can even guide him. Send him my message."

Sending Jerome a peace message would signal my
death. Even if the colonel would be satisfied to call
off his hounds from Noah, I wouldn't last one minute.

Looking at failure eyeball to eyeball was bad
enough. I hated it like hell. But it was worse imagin-
ing what would happen to my hide with Jerome as
vindictive as I believed. It was a good hide. There
were some patches on it, but the seals were tight. So
far. I waited sourly for the patriarch's reaction to
Fleming's offer. It came in a weary tirade.

"Doctor, I respect your idealism but it is blinding
you. When General Hammond deposed you, the people still believed his promises to keep Grand LaClare
Island for the islanders. He could afford to exile you.
Carib Jerome cannot be so generous. He is as unpo-
pular as he is ambitious. You are a threat to him so
long as the population could be rallied to you.

"It is not only your life that's at stake but ours
too. If Jerome succeeds, he plans to use this place as
a missile site, drive us away and move our enemies
in. He cannot hold power without Communist backing. This mountain has been our sanctuary, our
home, for centuries. Our people will die fighting for
it."

The old bastard was glorious. He got to Fleming

too. The doctor showed his guts, squared himself, and said, "I can't fault your logic, Noah. I have dreamed too long. Hope is a seductive temptress, isn't she? Well, I can throw stones with one hand."

He touched Noah's arm in a lingering gesture of affection, then turned and hobbled toward the stairs leading to the sea.

Noah winked at me.

I climbed to the roof and looked through a crenel to the mouth of the cove. The fleet coming through it reminded me of the one that had evacuated the British from Dunkirk in World War II. I think every fishing boat from Port of Spain, anything that would float, was massed around the headland, waiting for room to come through the channel. There were little boats with lateen sails designed to take tourists into the big harbor at the capital to watch the natives dive for coins. There was the lubberly craft in which vacationing anglers went after the wahoo, that brilliant fish that lost its bright colors almost as soon as it came out of the water.

There were yachts and outboards leading the pack, more than fifty in all, all crowded with men in uniforms.

I daydreamed of a couple of U.S. destroyers and of some air cover showing up over the horizon. It was a nice daydream.

The lead boats were well into the cove now, a rank of them making toward the shore at wide intervals. Those farthest away would make it. The rest had a surprise ahead. They came at full speed, unbelievably innocent of the breakwater they would run into. Noah's reputation must have kept everyone away from this small harbor so that knowledge of the stone teeth under the surface was lost.

I watched two yachts running neck and neck. Even without binoculars I could see the bazookas and machine guns cradled by the men on deck. They hit the breakwater at the same time with a grinding shriek of metal. The prows heaved into the air. The hulls shuddered, the sharp bottoms rolled, the impact shooting men and weapons high and flinging them into the sea.

As if to punctuate that grand slam, Mitzy's first charge of dynamite roared from the trail.

Behind the yachts two tugs with too much momentum to stop in time struck the hidden wall. They rammed onto the rock and hung there, balanced on their mid sections, men tumbling overboard to flail in the water. Some of them sank, weighed down by boots and guns. Others found the stone and hung to it, stunned. The next line of boats hove to, veered back toward the middle of the cove and lay there. But three scows heavily loaded with soldiers chugged close along the base of the headland, probing with poles and came against the breakwater where it joined the steps leading to the fort. The men from the first boat started up. The third scow backed off and threw a screen of lead at the top of the parapet.

I hadn't seen Noah scramble up a ladder, but there he was beside me now, crouched to keep his head low one eye against a bamboo periscope built with an extra mirror to look directly down. He had one hand raised to signal. All along the wall brown figures waited, watching him, each man holding a stone.

I heard the soldiers' boots, the noise growing above the machine gun fire from the scow. Then I heard a wheezing grunt beyond the wall, and the soldiers were just below us. Noah slashed his hand down. There was flurry at the crenels. Men ignored the guns shooting at them, bent over the three-foot-thick wall, slammed their stones down and slipped back to shelter. Three fell back, bloodied. Others dragged them away and took their places.

The covering fire stopped abruptly. I looked through the crenel at the head of the steps. I was in time to see soldiers flying through the air, falling toward the sea—a domino ripple of bodies knocking each other down the stairs. They piled up at the bottom or rolled off to the water.

Noah's men picked up more rocks, ready for another attack. The shock that had stopped the firing wore off and lead again sailed through the apertures and slapped into the wall.

NINE

A second muffled explosion shook the jungle, Mitzy had to blow another charge. Noah didn't need me at the moment. The Luger couldn't reach a boat, and their guns weren't damaging the wall too much now. The old giant had the steps under control. I ran for the trail. Mitzy squatted on the ground, holding the third fuse and looking perplexed.

"They got smart in a hurry," she told me. "I caught seven the first time and four the next, bunched together. Now they're coming one at a time, twenty feet apart. It's a waste, a whole charge for only one man."

"It sure is, so hold it. I can handle them one by one."

The soldiers were coming up unenthusiastically but still coming, bullied by officers bawling at their rear. They weren't looking up the grade but swiveling their heads side to side, watching the ground before them to spot booby traps.

I fought down through the scrub brush where the trail dropped out of sight behind the nose of a rock. If I could make that spot before a soldier appeared, I would be in range to pick them off with the Luger as they came around. I had barely gotten there when the first man walked into sight. He was short, very dark, his face streaming sweat. He stopped to pant, then came on, moving slowly, eyes on the trail. I lifted the Luger, then lowered and holstered it. There was a better way. He didn't know I was there.

My ammo was already in too damn short supply, and there was no gun shop handy. I shook the stiletto out of the arm sheath; when the soldier came under me, I leaped on his back. He bent forward. My feet hit his spine hard. He went on his face, flat, the air driven out of him. Normally I don't kill unconscious men, but one luxury I couldn't afford now was taking prisoners. I cut his throat, cut off his cartridges, kicked him into the downhill brush, took his rifle and sprinted around back to my nest. If my wind held out, I could take the lot of them and also stockpile a lot of arms. Nice.

The next man turned the bend and stopped, eyes following the trail up. He looked startled when he saw the blood in the dirt. His head lifted higher, turned, and he looked into my face. He carried a machine gun across his belly. It swung toward me. This one was not for knives. I snapped out the Luger and blew his head apart.

He fell only three or four steps from the blind bend in the road. But I wanted that machine gun. With the Luger in my hand, I dropped down, sprinted to the body and, my eyes on the path, worked quickly. He not only had the ammunition loop in the gun but two more over his shoulders. A gold mine. I slipped those off, rolled the soldier over the edge into the brush, gathered up my prizes, and ran.

Nobody came around the bend. Not while I was on the trail. Not while I settled down to wait for another target. Time ran on. They must have stopped when they heard the Luger. I stayed on for fifteen more minutes, but no one had showed. I went up to Mitzy with my load. From there I looked down on the truck and the jeeps. The soldiers were straggling down the trail, gathering around a man with a walkie-talkie who was looking uphill. He wanted new orders from somebody higher up in the chain of command. Mitzy whistled in appreciation of our new guns. I grinned at her.

"They won't stop everything Jerome can throw at us, but they'll put a dent in the front. This army will know it's been somewhere." I indicated the group at the bottom. "They're changing plans. The trail's too tough and I think they won't try a frontal advance again. Stay here and watch and come tell me if I'm wrong."

Her tongue darted out and around her lips. She said, "Leave me the rifle, will you? I may get a chance to do some hunting. Head hunting."

I left her the rifle and the cartridges. I went off in a hurry, hearing another sound— a sort of growl on the shore highway. It was time to get ready for more dynamite.

I was ready with the fuses when the new cars stopped at the road's end and men tumbled out. A walkie-talkie was being used in the lead car, so these soldiers wouldn't advance in a bunch. I didn't wait for them to separate but got the first charge on its way. It went off under a jeep and took two carloads with it. When it was quiet, I poured a burst from the machine gun into the next row of cars. Those still functioning slammed into reverse for a discretionary retreat, out of range. It looked as if they'd stay back awhile, so I headed into the fortress.

It was noisy on the roof. Everybody kept down while bazookas and long-range guns raked the parapet. Noah beckoned to me for a look through his bamboo peeper. By now the soldiers had discovered the breakwater, found where it ran under the surface, and were nursing men from along it toward the steps. Some of these had reached the wall and were starting up. Noah's mouth turned down.

I used the viewer again. Under cover of the heavy barrage, a line of soldiers was climbing toward us. In a few minutes the boats would be picking off their own people if they kept shooting. But at the moment the firing was too heavy for another rock party. I patted the machine gun and told Noah, "Tell me when they're near the top."

I needn't have asked. The covering fire quit abruptly so it wouldn't hit the men on the stairs. That was all the cue I needed. I heard a rush of boots as I stepped through the crenel. There was a rifle almost in my face but it wavered as the soldier humped for the next step. A burst from the machine gun blew him back into the man below. Both of them went over the edge. I sprayed the stairs, cleared it and the breakwater within range. The men beyond turned, headed back to the boats, slipping, falling, tumbling into the crafts. There wasn't any more shooting. The flotilla withdrew around the far end of the breakwater and beached in the part of the cove where Mitzy and I had discovered each other in the salty water. It seemed a lifetime ago. I went back to Noah, crouched and lit a cigarette, one of those long, thin, good tasting joys made for me in Istanbul.

"That's act one," I said. "We can rest for awhile."

"You may rest, Nick. My thanks for all you've done. But the siege is not broken, only halted for a short while. Jerome's army will be back. I know my people think they have won and they expect a celebration. If they do not have one, they will accuse me of neglecting to thank the gods so that they abandon us. Then they'll lose the will to fight again, and other battles are coming."

Noah left me for the "victory" party, with sacred fire, drums, dancing. I divided my time between watching the ritual and checking the cove. Most of the boats were beached; it surprised me to see that the soldiers kept close to them and didn't head for the fortress. The walkie-talkies must be burning the air with orders and counter orders.

I was looking down toward the water when a hand crept into mine, smooth, warm, tightening on my fingers. I turned my head. A girl bent over me, naked from the waist up, skin shining from the celebration dance. Her breasts swayed against my face. My breath became ragged. That wasn't all that happened to me.

I ought to stay on watch. Nobody else was. But those damn drums were pounding in my skull. And besides, there was no action from the boats. I climbed down the ladder behind her. We came together on a soft couch of leaves, just beyond the gate.

Then it was over. Now the drums were muted. I heard a prayer in them and I felt a strange peace. I lifted the girl to her feet and we walked back, hand in hand. I left her to climb the ladder and looked through the crenel again.

The fleet was moving out into the open sea. Only one straggler was still inside the harbor maneuvering through the channel entrance.

Nuts. What the hell was happening?

I went down to talk to Noah who stood with Fleming and Tara. I gave them the news.

"Now we can spirit the doctor and the girls out of here," I said. With some muscle, we can run for another island where I can get word out to America to send us a plane. That way at least the doctor can stay alive for another try. And I can come back later to liquidate the colonel."

But Fleming wouldn't hear of it. He dug in his heels and said he'd never accept a post he owed to the United States. No planes. And no me to get rid of Jerome. I gave up, said sourly that it was his business. Mine was only to save all our hides. He and Noah could have it out while I got the wrecked boats off the rocks.

Noah chose some men to help me. The best swimmers, he said. I didn't need swimmers. I needed a floating crane. I asked the old giant to have his men cut strong poles, and he sent them out with machetes. I used the time to learn how Mitzy was doing.

Mitzy sat where I left her, but the jeeps below

were gone. Only the truck was still there. She said they'd pulled out in a bunch; the timing would make the withdrawal about the same time that the cove had emptied. I told her the boats left and so had the force on the shore highway. She looked skeptical.

"You don't think Jerome is really giving up, do you? What's he doing?"

I hadn't mentioned to Noah and Fleming what I really thought. But I could talk to Mitzy.

"I'd say he's yelling for help from Castro. You're going to see bombers and gunboats and whatever else Russia can send by way of Cuba. I hope we won't be here by then." I also told her about the boats on the breakwater and that I would advise Noah to send his tribe for a vacation somewhere else as soon as we left.

She gave me a sidewise look. "Mission impossible. Good luck."

TEN

I heard machetes chopping as I returned. Neither
Noah, Tara Sawyer nor Fleming were in sight. I assumed they were in a huddle somewhere, putting
pressure on the doctor to accept U.S. aid since that
was the possible way he could keep Russian missiles
away from Grand LaClare Island. I wished them
luck, just like Mitzy had wished me.

It was a while before Noah's men came through
the gate, bringing two long, straight, heavy tree
trunks. All twelve were needed to carry the logs, one
at a time. They lugged them up the ladder, slid them
through the slots and let them drop to the sea. Then
they brought coils of rope from a storehouse. I took
the machine gun and ammo belts and led the crew
down the steps.

The logs stood on end, only a foot showing above
the surface of the water, leaning against the cliff.
Swimmers dived off the bottom step, pulled a line
around the closest one, and came back. I led them all
across the breakwater, careful where I walked. If the
gun got a soaking, it might as well be thrown away.

The men kept losing their footing, hauling on the
line falling off the breakwater. The log had butted
deep into the sand and it was a big job dragging it
free. When it came loose, the whole crew took a bath.

The log sank. They towed it, following my steps, maneuvering on the underwater stone. Any moment now Russian bombers could wing in overhead but I didn't mention that fact. There was nothing to gain.

The closest vessel, a yacht, lay hull over, stern in the water, the power plant dry. I had hope for it until I saw that the fiberglass bottom was gone. The men detoured the log around it, swimming, bouncing it along the sand. I climbed over the boat and went to the next one. That was bashed in worse than the first. Two tugs were left, built of metal so they should be whole.

Several brown bodies floated nearby drifting out to sea, small spots against the blue water. I left Noah's men working to get around the yachts and went to investigate the nearer tug. I slung the machine gun and belts aboard with the Luger and crouched to feel around. By the time the log came, I had found what I wanted and sent the men back for the second beam. While they were gone, I climbed into the cabin and tried the little diesel. It coughed and caught. I put it in reverse to test how solid the boat was hung up. The engine whined, the water churned, but the hull didn't budge.

When the crew came back, I showed them where we could get leverage, lined them up along the breakwater, and we set to work on either side of the hull. Six of them went up on each trunk. The prow lifted some. The men bounced the logs in a slow rhythm. The boat rocked. I started the engine and tried reverse again. The hull shuddered. Metal screamed against rock. Then one pry snapped. The boat rolled against the stub and hung there. The men were all dropped into the water.

It had been close. Another couple of minutes and power would have floated the craft. I shut down the engine to conserve fuel. Whatever was in the tanks was all we had for the run to another island. I doubted if Noah could come up with hose to siphon off fuel from the other tug.

The men clustered around the broken log, pulling loose the short stub. There was enough length left to use, but they hit a snag. It was too thick to wedge under the hull. I sent one man back for a machete and we waited. I watched the sky and the harbor mouth, listening for the drone of planes or gunboats.

When we had the knife, they whittled the log down to fit it in the crack between boat and stone. Then the crew was moving again and I started the engine.

The hull rocked, metal screamed once more, kept on screaming, and with a lurch the boat was free. I killed the engine. The timbers had twisted away and the crew was grinning in victory. I stood for a moment cheering them, then a bubbling sound turned me around. Down in the engine pit a fountain was gurgling, drowning the machinery. The water was rising fast, sinking the boat.

I jumped for the machine gun, and Luger belts, waved them at a man, indicating with sign language that the stuff shouldn't get wet. He lunged for the boat, took weapons and bullets, and passed them back. They were held high overhead until they reached the men on the breakwater.

We were down to the last boat. This time, before

we put any work on it, I investigated the interior and went underneath feeling for damage. There didn't seem to be any. But where this vessel hung, the wall had a sharp, jagged edge that would tear a gash when the hull skidded backward. We needed some kind of shield.

Before we did anything, I had to check the power plant. This tug had a converted four-cylinder Dodge motor. I climbed into the pit to crank it, threw it past compression six times, then quit. A gasoline engine that won't turn over in that time probably won't if you crank all day. I could think of four reasons why it wouldn't work. It was out of gas; it wasn't getting a spark; it had bad connections; it was just plain cursed with the perversity of inanimate objects. This one had gas, the tanks were nearly full, and the connections were tight. But when I fished a wrench from the tool box and pulled the plugs, I wondered how the skipper had got it started the last time. They were filthy, crusted with carbon. I used the stiletto to ream them out. The points on one were burned, the spread too wide. There was no gauge in the box so I had to guess about their usability. I bent them in with a screwdriver and hoped for the best. I screwed the plug back, waved the men out of the way, and gave the crank another whirl. It fired but did not catch. The same on the second yank. If the third didn't take hold, we were probably stranded.

The thought of losing Fleming burned me most. He was a selfless man with a life dedicated to bringing his people out of generations of exploitation. I could fault his bullheadedness, but not his vision. I talked to the engine in several languages. Funny superstition, that. Somebody answered. The next crank generated life. The beast took off in a rattle and clatter, coughed blue smoke, and settled into a steady roar. I let it burn out the gas that choked it, then shut it down.

It was time to consider protection for the hull. There was the jeep I'd left on the shore road. I swam for that, kicked around through the brush and vines, and came up with two flat chunks of hood I thought would fit. I took them back by way of the breakwater.

What I had in mind could get at least two of us killed. I didn't like asking the men to risk it, but there wasn't any choice. One of them spoke a few words of English. I explained then showed him what we had to do. I took him and one of the hoods under the boat with me to show that if the boat was rocked sideways on its keel, the metal piece could be laid over the ragged rock edge; the same could be done on the other side. But the hoods would have to be held there by hand until the weight of the boat slid over the metal. My man would have to hang in the water, under the wall, with one arm on top to be mangled if the hull tipped. He could be trapped there, his body crushed, if the prow dropped.

I gave it to him without frills when we surfaced. He thought it over, looked up at the fortress, swallowed, and volunteered.

We got ready. Noah's man and I dropped off the breakwater with the plates. The men on top rocked the boat to one side, then the other; we set the metal pieces and surfaced to signal that all was ready. Then we dropped under again. With one hand on the plate to hold it from twisting off and the other on the hull, I felt the boat shudder as the crew climbed the logs. The vessel tilted, then quickly righted before it hit my arm. The men bounced up and down. The craft moved grudgingly, then in a swift glide it came down on us.

I got my hand away and dived to the side. The stubby prow raked my foot, then I was clear. The boat was floating on the water. I went under to see about the man on the far side. His brown legs were kicking upward at an angle. When I broke the water, he was perched on the wall with a grin, holding up two whole hands.

But the others weren't laughing. They were scrambling for the breakwater and yelling. The man who'd been with me straightened suddenly, looked out at the cove, then yelled.

"Shark."

I spun. The sharp dorsal fin was close, cutting toward me. I heard my man dive, shouting as he went under. The fin did a U-turn and swam in a wide circle, slowing. Then the man was up again, rushing toward the breakwater. Those already on it had the tug alongside, piling onto it. We scrambled aboard and I reached for the machine gun. The fin came back, cruised past and I gave it a burst. The dark shape rolled over, showing the white belly and the vicious mouth. Blood spread through the water.

I put the gun down to start the engine, but another shout stopped me. The water boiled with barracuda

drawn by the dead shark's blood. I remembered the
floating bodies. They too must have bled, attracting
the voracious fish from the open sea. There had been
no sign of such killers when Mitzy and I had been in
these waters. And the girl, who'd swum here dozens
of times, had never mentioned them either.

We didn't stay to watch the carcass being stripped, but chugged to the steps, moored the tug,
and climbed. I kept the guns with me, not knowing
what I'd find at the top. We hadn't heard any shooting but, Jerome's army could've forced an entrance
anyway.

They had not. Tara was alone on the roof, watching us.

"Anything new up here?" I asked.

"Everyone's getting ready to leave. Noah wants
his people on the other side of the mountains, scat-
tered in the jungle, where Jerome can't dig them out.
He's gone to bring back Mitzy."

Fleming sat in a chair below us, beside a lot of
baskets filled with food. There looked to be enough
for a voyage to the mainland instead of a few hours
of island hopping.

Noah and Mitzy came through the gate, the girl
lugging the rifle. The old patriarch looked worried.

"Is there enough fuel to take you to a safe shore?"
When I nodded, he added, "Go quickly then while
the route is open. I hope you do not have trouble on
the water." He raised his voice, called for porters to
put the baskets in the boat, then reached for Fleming's hand.

The doctor didn't give it. He sat straight and determined. "Unless you come with us, old friend, I will not leave."

Noah was exasperated. "You don't expect me to abandon my people now, do you?"

Arguments cost time. I took Fleming's hand. "Noah, your people will be all right. Jerome could never dig them out. But he knows you're harboring the doctor and you'll be a special target."

There was a sad smile from the old man and another bluster from Fleming.

"He is absolutely right. You are too valuable. Come with us and we will return together.

At least, Fleming had agreed that he must leave. Now he and Noah glared at each other while precious minutes flicked by. I gestured to the girls to head for the boat, leveled the machine gun on Noah and told him flatly, "You're going to get yourself killed one way or another. Balk any longer and I'll knock a leg out from under you."

I knew I'd never do it, but Noah couldn't be sure. More peaceful souls than I had been known to lose their heads and do crazy things during moments of stress. And this was as stressful as it could get. Noah nodded assent.

He swung around to his people, thundering commands. They filed by him, listening obediently. The girls and I went down to the tug. We waited. And waited. I was back on the steps, heading up, when Noah finally showed, carrying Fleming.

I had the engine running when he stepped aboard. I'd already cast off before he found a place for the doctor and was heading across the cove toward the open sea.

ELEVEN

There was a headwind, enough to ruffle the surface of the water, but not strong enough to slow us. We were slow enough at full throttle. This was no racing craft. It was designed to tow the barges that ferried the produce of the back country to the port at the capital. At the speed we were going, it was going to be an overnight cruise to even the closest island. In the bright sunshine we were a sitting duck if enemy planes showed up before we cleared the cove. Once we were outside I could hug the shore and maybe escape being seen, then make the run across the open sea at a place where they wouldn't expect us to be. The shoals were shallow all through these parts, but I was pretty certain we wouldn't find any more subsurface walkways. If we were spotted, we'd had it.

I was following the contour of the cove, ragged at this end with dense jungle growth all the way to the water. The limestone dropped off to an undersea canyon. Judging water depth by its color, I kept as close to the shore as I dared, hoping the tug would blend in with the dark foliage. It didn't work.

We had almost made it when the plane came. He came in low and slow, sideslipping in the air current flowing over the ridge, spotted us only after he was practically on top of us and banked away for a sweeping circle. Then he dropped even lower and came at us.

He wouldn't be carrying bombs, but he was armed with something or he wouldn't be making this run. The little workhorse I was commanding had good maneuverability and I tried weaving in and out. Noah shoved Fleming into the pilot house with me, pushed Tara onto the deck, and lay on top of her.

Fast lead spit a path toward us in the water. I spun the wheel and the bullets spattered past. I heard our machine gun chatter as the plane went over us for the second time. Grabbing a look toward the stern, I saw Mitzy standing, tracking the plane, the gun jerking in her hands.

She got a hit too. A wing tank exploded, tore apart. The ship peeled off and disappeared into the water. Mitzy put the gun down and tossed me a victory sign. I didn't feel like cheering yet. The spotter probably was in radio contact with the small plane; if the pilot got a message in, there'd be others along soon with more clout. Still, they weren't in sight yet and we wouldn't sit here waiting for them.

At the mouth of the cove the sand bottom rushed up toward us. But the tug had a shallow draft and we slipped over without dragging. I made the curve around the land nose into open sea. As soon as we rounded it, I saw them—a pair of patrol boats frothing at the knife prow. Sleek greyhounds with bared fangs ready to run down a wallowing turtle. Our four cylinder Dodge was not going to outdistance their big power plants.

All we could do was buy time. Chase back to the doubtful sanctuary of the fortress? I didn't know if we could make it. I turned the tug around and called behind me.

"Anybody here know how to run a boat?"

Both girls did. They'd only been on yachts, of course, but the tug handled the same way.

"Take over here. Go on back up. We'll have to wait for dark to try again."

Tara slid past Fleming, reached for the wheel saying tightly, "They're too fast, Nick. We can't make it."

"Sure you will. Keep the faith."

There wasn't time for explanations. I jumped for the stern, grabbed the machine gun and ammo and dropped over the side. I waded to shore and dived into the jungle, climbing the sharp rise. The tug lumbered on taking the direct route. The patrols turned and their bow guns reached ahead. Little fountains popped up just short of our boat.

They were in too big a hurry, staying in the wake of the tug, running side by side. Lousy pilots. They jolted and bucked, grounded on the sandbar and hung. Everyone on board fell down. I was above them with the closer one in my range. My gun swept the deck, knocked the gunner over the rail, cut across the glass bridge and dropped both men there.

The second patrol was out of machine gun reach but I wasn't out of theirs. I moved. They didn't know just where I was, but both their long-range guns sent bullets peppering through the trees to find me. I stood behind a thick trunk waiting for them to get tired or run out of lead. Whichever it was, it didn't take long. They had a bigger problem than a machine gun on a hill that couldn't touch them.

The throb of their engine revved up to a high pitch, trying to back off the bar. The stern moved from side to side. All except the pilot went overboard to shove on the sharp prow. The boat moved an inch at a time, then it floated, the crew swung back on her and she crawled for deeper water. She turned toward Port of Spain and disappeared behind the far headland.

I went down to the shore where I could see along the cove. Our boat reached the cliff and everyone was on the steps, going up. I thought I had a nice surprise for them. If one patrol boat could be freed from the sandbar so easily, I should be able to float the other. We could leave Grand LaClare in style. And if some of us borrowed the crew's uniforms, anybody seeing us at sea would take us for a part of Jerome's fleet. There would be no problem in floating the vessel. I planned to go on foot to the fortress, pick up my people and bring the tug here. If it had enough power to haul barges, it had the power to tow the patrol boat off the sand. I felt very good indeed.

Until I heard the voices. And the crunch of boots uphill from me.

There were men up there, four or five at least, beating the jungle, calling to each other. Where the hell had they come from? Did it matter? Obviously the gunfire had brought them. It was time for me to leave. I considered the dinghy on the patrol boat. But it wasn't smart to put out in the cove where they could see me. I could go down and swim under the cover of the overhanging brush. Sure. There was blood in the water again and there'd be more barracuda or sharks. What I needed was to get behind the soldiers, in an area they had already searched.

Edging toward the nose of land with as little sound as possible, I turned the corner, came out on top of a bluff, and saw open sea running against the shore. A third patrol boat lay close by and its dinghy was drawn up on a stretch of sand at a bottom of the hill. I guessed the boat carried a handful of men. If it had brought more, there would be many more voices in the searching party.

What to do now? Sit down and wait for the soldiers? The idea didn't appeal to me. By nature I'm a hunter. I don't like waiting for trouble to come to me. I go to it. A man on the offensive has the advantage. I had an extra edge here. Anyone I heard or saw had to be the enemy. Whatever movement or sound *they* caught, could be one of them. They would have to hold fire until they knew they weren't killing each other while I could zero in on anything I saw.

The only way to go was through their line. I had another edge in the density of growth here, a deep mat of tangle on the ground, a three-dimensional web of vine between the trees. Visability was only about thirty feet in any direction.

Cradling the machine gun so it wouldn't catch in the vine, I went with caution, keeping low, worming forward. Within a hundred feet something brown moved. A man with his back toward me crouched to go under a loop of vine, intent on something ahead.

He brushed through tall ferns and I lost sight of him. I went after him. If I could take him out, it would leave a hole in their line for me to go through. The noise of my shot would bring the others, but then he could turn at any second, see me and blast away. And he wasn't at knifing distance.

I switched the machine gun to my left hand, shook the stiletto down and stalked him. Ten feet behind him now. Then he turned, bringing up his gun as he faced me. I threw the knife. It buried in his throat, dropped him before he fired, and he crumpled without sound. I went to him and bent to retrieve the knife.

My head exploded.

I came to with drums pounding inside, looked up at the treetops and saw three ugly, happy faces above army uniforms. My arms were underneath me, tied tight. One of the three men was a sergeant, the others privates. The sergeant had my knife under his belt, the privates carried my machine gun and Luger. The sergeant saw my eyes open, came closer and lobbed a boot in my ribs.

"For Belmont," he growled and kicked me again.

Was it Belmont's throat that I'd opened? I expected my throat to be next. There was nothing I could do to prevent being shot if I kicked the sergeant's gut to keep him off me. He was big with a permanent lopsided grin that a scar the length of one cheek pulled up.

He rubbed his hands together, pleased with his catch. "Get up, Mr. One-Thousand-Dollars," he said. "You going to get me a promotion too."

I didn't move. Apparently I was worth more to them alive than dead. If they wanted me, let them do all the work. The sergeant snapped his fingers at the privates and jerked a thumb up. The pair took my elbows and hauled me to my feet. One put the Luger against my shoulderblade and shoved. Either I walked or the gun would break the shoulder. I walked.

They pointed me down toward the beach and the dinghy. The sergeant bellowed to the rest of his team to quit looking, he had me. Two voices answered and the men came thrashing through the tangle. They all gabbled in self-congratulation, then the sergeant delegated the newcomers to bring the dead man along, and we were on our way. The bearers of the corpse were in front of me, the privates on either side, and the sergeant brought up the rear. I didn't care much for my prospects. I figured I had a date with a dungeon and probable execution on any charge Carib Jerome chose to trump up. And even if Hawk should become aware of my fate, he couldn't lift a finger. He couldn't admit we had an agent involved in island politics.

Halfway to the beach, a gun spat from the jungle. A cry behind me turned us all around. The sergeant was no longer walking. He was toppling, a hole in the breast of his jacket.

The privates jumped as if to catch him, missed and swung their rifles, searching the dense growth for something to shoot at. The gun spat again and the private on my left went down, minus the back of his head. The one on my right spun, crouching, looked at the mess in astonishment and fright,, and began to run.

I put a foot between his legs and sent him sprawling. I booted him in the head lightly, but it was enough to knock him cold. The remaining two privates threw their hands high over their heads.

Mitzy wriggled through the vines, a revolver in her hand leveled at the pair. She shot one before I could get close enough to shove her wrist down. The other soldier kept his hands very high.

The girl looked at me angrily. "You squeamish, Carter? We haven't got time for prisoners." She rubbed her wrist but kept hold of the revolver, training it again on the man.

"Quit it," I said. "I want them alive." Keep this one covered and see if you can get the twine on my wrist untied with one hand."

I turned my back and she picked at the knot, got it loose and I worked my hands out of the bond. Working the cramp out of my fingers, I took the cord to the soldiers. With a swift, sure gesture I demonstrated that it would not be difficult to garrote them. They got the message.

My man was coming around, groggy, scared when he discovered he was trussed up, and not in a mood to argue my orders. He got up, clumsy with the load of lead on him, and the two soldiers followed me up the ridge and down to the shore with Mitzy riding herd behind.

The sleek craft still sat on the sandbar. We waded out and I stopped my muscle boys at the bow, took the girl to the stern and hoisted her to my shoulders.

Then, with me holding her ankles, she raised herself to where she could get a grip on the lower rail. She chinned up and over and went forward to the cabin.

The engine ground when she tried the ignition, caught, settled into a throaty purr and I waded forward. There was a cough, a sputter, and the noise died. The diagnosis was disaster. And I could thank myself for it.

"Cut the switch," I called to Mitzy.

I went over to be sure, jumped for the rail, hauled myself aboard and followed the holes traced by my machine gun. Sure enough, the fuel line was cut. Worse, the tank was punctured and dry. I stood looking down, feeling a heavy sag. No fuel, no power. No power, no patrol boat. We were back on the rock and there was no way—no way—to get off.

The girl yelled from the pilot house. "The soldiers, Nick. They're running away."

They were. I tossed a Luger shell in front of them. They stopped, waiting with hunched shoulders for a shot in the back. I dropped over the side and splashed to them. There was no use holding them any longer but I wanted the ammo they were wearing. I shoved them on to dry land, waving Mitzy after us. When she came up, I let her cover one man while I stripped boots and trousers off the other. I knotted the cuffs, filled the pants with bullets, cinched the waist tight with the belt and slung the legs around my neck.

"Turn them loose now," I told the girl. "We don't need them with the boat out of fuel and they can't do any more damage at this point. Two more or less won't make any difference." I waved them away.

They didn't need urging. When they were gone, the girl and I hiked to the fortress, climbed the hill behind it and went in through the gate.

Inside Noah had a supper fire going and fish broiling over the coals. My stomach reminded me how many meals it had missed. My back told me it had enough too. Although there was another job to do before dark, there was still a long twilight to come and time for a breather.

I made it to one of the rooms, got my heavy packet off and sank to the stone floor, letting the tension run out. Mitzy would tell where we'd been.

She brought me rum from somewhere, hot fish and fruits. I didn't know how high she was on David Hawk's list, but if some feat of magic pulled us out of this, I meant to go to bat for her. She deserved a special medal.

TWELVE

It was time to destroy the steps. They were no use to us any longer, now that escape by sea was out.

Obliterating such an archeological treasure was a step I hated to take, but it was too dangerous an access into the fortress. We would hear cars coming on the shore road and the mountain trail, but Jerome could send rowboats in the dark and slip his men up from the cove before we discovered them. There were too few of us to keep watch on all fronts.

There was pain in Noah's eyes when I told him what had to be done.

I opened the last box of dynamite, took out two sticks, caps and a length of fuse, and paused before the old patriarch.

"It hurts me too, Noah. If we get out of this alive, I promise you AXE will build you new stairs."

I took the machine gun down with me to the third lowest step, shot holes through the hard limestone crust and into the softer stuff that hadn't oxidized, placed the charges and lit the fuse. I went up on the double and was inside the wall when the explosion came. An avalanche of rubble splashed into the water, then the sound died. The cliff was a sheer drop once more.

That left the two trails to keep an eye on through

the night. Dr. Fleming looked well enough so Noah and I could haul him to another mountain when morning came. With the rest of my group joining Noah's people in hiding, I could sneak into the town, locate Jerome and notch another Killmaster mark on my holster. With the army's head cut off, things should simmer down and Fleming could be installed as president.

I put it up to Noah, would he go along with my plan? He would. Would he watch the shore road to-night while I took on the back trail? He would. We went down to the fuse and I showed him what it was about, told him the time limits involved and took off in the other direction. So long as the dynamite held, nobody was going to surprise us that night.

Tara declared herself in on the action. "My father sent me to help, you know. And you need rest. Don't you think I can light matches as well as Mitzy?"

Light matches, yes, but I didn't know how steady she would be under pressure. Still, her company would take the loneliness out of my vigil. I didn't really expect an attack in the dark. The colonel's forces had been bloodied considerably in the first assault. After the loss of the patrol boat, I figured Jerome would sit back, lick his wounds and wait for rescue.

I told the girl I'd take the first watch, but she wouldn't hear of it. She insisted I needed to relax. She wouldn't even play games. So I stretched out and went to sleep.

It was daylight when the sun in my eyes brought me awake. I felt whole again except for a dull ache and a lump on my head where the soldier had knocked me out. Tara sat with her back against a tree, awake but drowsy, dark circles halfway down her cheeks. I rolled toward her.

Her voice was hollow. "Nick, I'm sick, my stomach feels awful. It's been getting worse for the last couple of hours."

We were under the high arch of trees and shafts of yellow sunlight filtered through the leaves. The air was heavy with shadows. Tara's skin was green-white and shiny with perspiration. A dull filter glazed her eyes. I picked her up in my arms, running up the hill to the gate. I raced inside shouting for Noah, afraid he was still at his watch. For whatever it was worth, he was the only medicine man in town.

He came in just behind me. I placed Tara gently on the ground, and Noah took over. He touched the glands in her neck, touched her wrist, pried her mouth open caught her hands, holding the palms up. I saw blisters on her fingertips before he let them drop.

I had never seen the old man in such a rush before. He dashed for one of the rooms. I started after him, but before I made it to the door he was back, carrying a mat and an armful of gourds. He dropped the mat, kicked it flat and nodded at me to lay the girl on it. I realized he wanted light and couldn't waste time lighting torches in the dim rooms.

As I put Tara down, I peeled off her dress. Mitzy was suddenly there, curious as hell, but then she saw the blonde's bloodless lips and was on her knees to help.

Noah had half a gourd invisible in one big hand, shaking what appeared to be water and yellow soap into a foamy liquid.

"Move back." His words were sharp. When we did, he lifted Tara's head, pinched her mouth open, and poured the froth down her throat.

"Manchineel," he clipped out. "A highly poisonous tree. One taste of its fruit can mean sudden, painful death. Even touching the bark can be dangerous. Just look at this poor child."

Abruptly, violently Tara retched. Noah propped her against a knee and poured her full again. While she alternately swallowed, choked, and heaved, I remembered what I knew of manchineel. It was pretty bad, just like Noah said.

The old man needed help now. He said, "Pour a little of the mixture on her fingers. Don't rub them."

I did that. He whipped her up, hauled her over his knee on her stomach and we saw her back. It too was blistered where she had leaned against the bark of the tree. I dribbled the syrupy liquid over Tara's body and heard a sigh of relief from the old man.

"None of them broken. All right. She will be all right."

The convulsions eased off. Tara lay limply on the ground. Noah set down the soap mix, reached for other gourds, made a thick emulsion of white powder and what looked like honey, turned the girl and poured that into her. Then he laid her on her side.

"Now you." He stood up, examined my hands, unfastened my shirt and skinned it off inside out. I had carried her. The cloth was contaminated. He anoint-

ed my hands and his own with whatever the neutral-
izing agent was, giving me a rueful smile. "I should
have warned you. Most of the jungle is a friend but a
few things are not. Will you take one end of the mat
—we will carry her into the shade now."

Tara opened her eyes as we moved her into a dim
room. Fleming was already there with a bed of
fresh-cut boughs, hobbling on a crutch. I hadn't even
realized he was around. We laid Tara on the bed and
Mitzy brought a bright grass coverlet. Tara was con-
scious now, but still a very sick girl.

There would not be an exodus from the fort today.
We couldn't carry both Fleming and Tara over the
rough mountains. We would have to wait it out.

I stayed crouched beside the blonde girl, chewing
on frustration, more worried about Tara than I'd
liked to admit. She had gotten to me and her illness
made me realize it. If Noah hadn't recognized the
poison, she'd be dead by now instead of sleeping. The
old man had delivered on the dot.

Breakfast smells came through the door. I ignored
them until Noah called, then I went out to where the
others were gathered around the glowing brasier.

I had a surprise waiting. We had company.

A dark young man in a twist of cloth. He brought
news. Noah told it to me in a tired voice while Fleming and Mitzy looked depressed. The tribe had been
busy through the night, scouting. Carib Jerome's soldiers had been busy, too. There was now a cordon of
them from the shore of the cove all the way to the
beach where the third patrol boat lay.

We were encircled. With two people on the sick list, there wasn't a chance in hell of breaking through. I asked the boy if he could take me out for a try at Jerome when it got dark again. No, he said. He'd come in before the encirclement was completed. Now he couldn't get through.

Tara hadn't heard any movements. If I hadn't slept, I might have—or maybe they'd been too far away. I looked at the silent figures around me, realized what easy targets we made, and lost my appetite.

We ate anyway. It was something to do. Then we sat listening. The wait was not long. I heard it first, a split second before Noah turned his head to look at me. There was the low, lazy drone of planes coming out of the morning sun.

The old man stood up without hurry, sounding as if he were inviting us for tea. "I suggest we repair to the catacombs now. Mr. Carter, will you bring Miss Sawyer."

As Mitzy had said when I first met him, the old man was full of surprises. So he had a basement under his fortress. I wondered how deep it was, if the rock ceilings could withstand the bombs or if a hit on top would bury us below. Mitzy's color faded under her lustrous tan and I knew the same thing was going through her mind. But once again there wasn't much choice.

I went for Tara, lifted her and was relieved that she could put an arm around my neck. When I brought her outside, Noah was holding open a thick limestone slab, a door I hadn't spotted before. Mitzy and the kid were already out of sight, Felming was hunching through on his crutch. I followed. Noah pulled the slab closed, leaving us in utter darkness.

A second later he struck a spark from a flint against a candle wick. We had light. Noah handed the candle to the boy, took the doctor in his arms, and walked into a dark entrance of a tunnel, then down some steps. The boy beckoned to us, holding the little flame above his head. The space was wide enough for us to pass, but the roof was low. The tall man ahead bent double. I had to kink my knees and even Mitzy ducked her head.

It was a long flight down. Encouraging. There would be enough rock over us to absorb quite a jolt. At the bottom a sharp turn took us into a fair-sized chamber.

We settled down on the floor and Noah pinched the candle. To conserve air, he said. Minutes passed. The planes must have reached us by now, but no explosions shook the headland. There was no sound at all.

It was spooking me. What were they waiting for? Then I had a new idea. In our haste to get away from the bombs, we'd left ourselves no exit. It was quite possible that the air raid would slam shut the door of the catacombs, piling rubble againt it so it couldn't be moved. There was only one way we'd be sure to get out—with dynamite. And that had been left upstairs.

Mitzy had brought the machine gun and I felt for

it in the dark. I made my way up the stairs and eased
the slab door open about two inches. The bright daylight blinded me, but I thought I caught movement. I
stayed where I was until I could see clearly. Four figures in Russian uniforms materialized. Of course.
The colonel wanted Fleming alive, not blown into
fertilizer.

They had machine guns too. Climbing out of their
parachute harness, they separated, two starting one
way around the grounds, two the other, looking into
rooms. They evidently expected to find people there.
The search speeded up. They were all looking away
from me, going through houses on the opposite side. I
shoved the slab aside and stepped against the dark
wall. I'd made a bad mistake. If I'd waited above
ground I could have picked them off parchuting
through the air. Now I had to stay here and sweat it
out.

It was quite awhile before one of them put his
head around my door and looked into the muzzle of
my gun. The empty rooms had made him careless, his
gun was down. I motioned for him to come in and
stepped back. He didn't like the idea, but he came.
When we were well inside, out of sight, I slammed
my barrel against his head. He fell and didn't move.
I went back to the door.

The next man was backing out of a room around
the corner; close enough. I shook out the stiletto and
threw it. I don't often miss, but he turned. The blade
passed him, rang on the wall and clattered at his
feet. He stared, then swung my way but not until I

had moved back from the opening. He yelled to the others in rapid-fire Russian. An answer came from the other side of my door. They planned to come in blasting, spraying the place on their way. That suited me. I dropped down the catacomb stairs, figuring they wouldn't shoot low and was ready when they came, bullets leading them, one at a time through the entrance. I cut them in two before they quite firing so the sound could be taken for only their guns.

The echoes covered Mitzy's scramble behind me. Her voice panted at my shoulder.

"What's going on?"

"Visitors. Four of them, three here, one still loose."

I climbed to the door but couldn't see the fourth man. I'd let go a yell of triumph, but he didn't flush. The court yard was still. Too still. I didn't know where he was and could get my head blown off if I went out looking. I didn't believe he'd blunder in here now. Stalemate.

I kicked a Russian gun toward the girl and told her, "Check it for ammunition."

"Plenty."

"Keep your head down. I'll go back to ask if there's another way out. Maybe I can get to our friend by another route."

After I described the situation, Noah lighted the candle. The flame showed Fleming sitting quietly against the wall. Tara sat a few feet away. She looked better, but still dazed. The dark hole in the depth of the mountain, smelling of dust and stale air, wasn't exactly a recovery room. But I couldn't take her out until that fourth man was found.

Noah spoke to the boy who had ghosted through Jerome's army. The young man nodded and took the candle, waving me to follow. The faint light shone upon a painted screen hung behind a primitive altar. He lifted a corner of the screen, revealing a passage behind it, and went into it ahead of me. I hoped he knew where he was going. The stub of candle wouldn't last very long. We went down more steps to a lower, curving tunnel lined with recesses. Bits of candle were stuck in the walls, never more than two-or-three inches long. The air was foul. Then I saw why. Most of the recesses held human bones, hollow-eyed skulls behind them on stone shelves. This was the burial crypt of the tribe.

The corridor was long with several turns. My sense of direction told me it led to the far side of the fortress. Finally there was a round pool of sunlight on the floor. Looking up, I saw a small hole in the roof, barely wide enough for my shoulders and too high for me to reach.

The boy understood. He reached for the machine gun, laid it and the candle on the floor, and offered his back for me to climb. I reached up, got my hands spread on the upper surface of the opening and lifted myself out.

I rested for a moment. I was on the roof of the rooms near the outer wall. The grounds appeared to be empty. I stretched an arm back down the shaft and felt the barrel of the gun the boy was handing up to me. I pulled it out, hearing the slap of his bare feet running down the tunnel. He was heading back to Noah.

Crawling to the edge of the roof I discovered my missing man, the fourth Russian—on his stomach behind the parachutes, his gun ready on the door behind which Mitzy watched. He wasn't far away. As individuals, the enemy are never impressive. This one was young, slight, but dangerous because of the lethal toy in his hands. I called to him in Russian, wanting him to face me.

"Up here."

He turned. I fired. He jerked and rolled. Mitzy appeared at the door, saw the body and walked toward it. I jumped off the roof.

In that fraction of time a fifth parachutist lunged from behind an open door, ramming a heavy revolver against Mitzy's neck. To kill him I'd have to shoot through her. He was looking at me.

He called in fair English, "Throw away the gun." Then he said something to the girl.

I let my gun fall. He gave an order: "Come this way, not close. Stand against the wall facing it."

I crossed past them. His uniform was of better material, better tailored than what the others wore. He had the mark of an officer and a walkie-talkie hung from his belt.

Even at the distance I could hear Mitzy's ragged breathing. He held her tighter and she gagged.

He laughed. "One chance for you both. Tell me where Dr. Fleming is. If you don't, I shoot first her, then you."

My stiletto was on the floor out of reach.

Mitzy's voice rasped through her teeth. "Tell him to go to hell."

I turned slowly, not to startle him. He cursed me. "I didn't tell you to move."

I pretended to be frightened. It was easy. I chattered, "Don't shoot. I'll tell you. He's hiding. I'll get him."

Mitzy swore at me, a thorough job. But I knew that if I could pass the catacomb's door, I'd find guns there. It didn't come off. The Russian knew they were there too. I could practically see the wheels turning in his head. He could use both Mitzy and me as a shield and walk to where I'd pointed. Then, using us as protection, he'd demand that Fleming give up. But suppose Fleming didn't give a damn about our lives and shot through us to get to the enemy? That was a possibility he couldn't risk.

So he tried another tack. He'd realized Mitzy was important to me by the way I laid down my gun the minute he'd grabbed her. He sneered.

"Yes. Go bring him. If there is a trick, the woman dies at once."

I had to play it out. He was a head taller than the girl and I trusted my aim with the Luger to blow his block off while he watched the door I'd gone through.

"Walk slowly," he told me. "With your hands high. Do not bend down. I will watch."

We marched toward the catacombs. Just before I reached the steps he told me to stop, wanting to accustom his eyes to the change of light; then he told me to go on. He didn't follow me any further. The stairs and the chamber below me felt like I was walking in India ink A soft footfall preceded me and at the bottom a hand was laid on my arm. Noah's voice whispered against my ear.

"I saw and heard. Come with me."

He kept hold of me, steering me ahead of him. I whispered to him what I had in mind, and his fingers tightened on my wrist.

"It will not work. You could not see behind you. There is too much risk that he would see a shadow in time to pull the trigger. We will try another way."

The word "shadow" gave Noah an idea. At least that's what he told me. He lit a candle, the glow dim in the large room. The light fell on an open box filled with small wooden dolls. Noah picked out one, pierced its chest with a long thin needle he'd also found in the box, then held it high in the air. His lips moved in silent prayer.

Good lord—all this while Mitzy stood outside with a nervous soldier aiming a gun at her neck.

The old man presented his prize for approval to me, walked around in a circle, and padded toward the stairs.

I had a glance at Tara's wide eyes and open mouth and of Fleming's expressionless face. I trailed along after Noah. This I had to see. Besides, I had to free Mitzy and she was where the old man was heading.

Mitzy and the soldier were standing in the gloom just behind the door, both of them in shadow. Noah and I stopped far enough down the steps to be out of sight. I watched the Russian's head turn from the stairwell to the outer door. Mitzy was angled between them, easy to pivot toward one or the other. I groaned without sound. No way. No way at all to take that sharpie by surprise.

The old man tossed the doll. It landed with a tiny click on the stone in the beam of sunlight. The man's head snapped toward the sound. I expected a shot right then to break the girl's spine. There was none. There was a frozen moment while I cursed Noah under my breath. No trick, the Russian'd warned. Without any doubt, that doll on its back, propped up by the needle point through its back, was the trick of the century.

There was a sudden violent movement in the shade. Both the man's arms were flung wide, his fingers spread as though an electric current had slammed through him. The gun clattered to the floor. He staggered back, made a convulsive grab at his chest with both hands, twisted, then curled down into a limp heap and didn't move again.

Mitzy had scooped up the gun before I got there. She stood with it hanging at her side, looking from the soldier to the doll. I rolled the man over. He was dead. His face a grimace of pain, eyes bulging. The classic look of a massive heart attack.

Here was a man on a new edge of nerves, killed by fear. I knew it. I was positive of it. Of course I was. A soldier who'd seen four friends killed in an ancient pirate stronghold reeking of legend. A man all alone with enemies. Tense to the breaking point. And out of nowhere flies a symbol of death, landing at his feet. Why wouldn't his heart stop?

It couldn't but did it? I looked at Noah.

The old man was busy with the bodies. He dragged the five dead soldiers over by the parachutes. Two lay against the pile of cloth, ankles crossed, arms folded behind their heads. The third was propped against the wall, knees folded, arms crossed, his head resting on his hands. The fourth was arranged the same way, and the officer sat in the woven chair Fleming had used. They presented the picture of a group that had successfully completed its mission and was now resting, waiting.

I got the message. If Fleming had been taken prisoner, he'd have to be taken away. The detail would have to be picked up too. There would be a helicopter along soon. Very good. Let it come. Let it put down here. The pilot would be alone since all available room would be needed for the passengers. I could handle him and we'd have wings. All I needed was the walkie-talkie on the officer's belt.

I went for it. Noah finished working, straightened and studied the sky. He drew a deep breath. He made a full turn, sniffing, then smiled.

"Wind is coming. It may help us later if we should need it."

He passed with a sidelong look that dared me to challenge his voodoo performance. Then he headed for the catacomb. Mitzy and I waited for the plane.

It was a half hour before we heard the flap of the chopper. It came over, circled, shredding air, and a rattle of Russian spat out of the microphone. He wanted to know if the doctor was in hand. I didn't have to lie in answering. I said Fleming was alive and we had him. The pilot laughed, broke contact and began to come down.

Tilting, tipping, tail swinging a little as he maneuvered the air drafts, the bird sank to the ground. Then the unforeseen happened. The prop wash blasted against the floor, ballooned out and blew the sitting bodies over on their sides.

The motor revved up. The ship lifted. It was over my head when I stepped out of the doorway, the pilot out of sight behind the belly. I couldn't get a shot at him. Even if I could, at that height he would wreck the plane. I let go a burst anyway, drawing a line the length of the underside. It didn't kill the pilot. He peeled up over the wall, disappearing behind it. I ran to look through the gun slots and saw the chopper drop into the cove in flames.

Beside me Mitzy taught me words I'd never heard.

We went downstairs. A candle was burning, reflected in all the anxious eyes. I shook my head.

"He got wise. We should've anchored those decoys. Noah, I guess your wind is about our last friend."

It was unkind to shaft him that way. I started an apology, but he held up a hand. He was quiet, unsmiling for a long minute, then his brows lifted, wrinkling the high forehead. There was a long sigh.

"Storms in winter are rare here. We expect them in June, July, particularly in August. However, it does no harm to ask. If the rest of you will leave me, I will make preparations for the ceremony."

Well, hell, we might as well have a show. It would pass time until Jerome threw his next wave at us.

Fleming accepted my arm to steady himself as he hopped up the steps behind the girls and the young native. Noah called after us.

"Please clear away bodies. They are offensive to the gods." The sudden malevolance in his voice was a shock.

I dumped the officer from Fleming's chair, let the doctor sink into it, and took the corpses to the corner turret. It was work wedging them through the slots, but by shoving them through head first, I managed to dump them into the sea. Then I went to sit beside Fleming.

Suddenly Noah appeared. He didn't look like the same man. His head was turbaned, amulets hung around his neck, long earrings swung from his lobes, bracelets covered half his forearms, gourds hung on a belt making hollow music as he walked. His eyes were wide open, staring, black depths with no bottom. He was high on something. He didn't see any of us, stalked to a ladder and climbed to the roof.

Up there he began to chant and dance, gourds bouncing, bracelets clinking, amulets flying, building to a pitch of frenzy. He spread his long legs, threw his head back and raised his arms to the sky. Wind, more than had been earlier, caught his white hair and beard, flailing them around his head. The voice I had guessed could thunder thundered now.

He stood, listening. Something answered. At first I thought it was a long, distant roll of thunder. A chill went through me. But it wasn't thunder and I had another chill. The sound was planes. Bombers. Coming high.

It appeared to me that Jerome's allies had given up on taking Fleming alive. The doctor was no use to them, only an obstacle to be swept aside to give them access to the island.

I saw the planes above the parapet, perhaps two miles away. This was no place to linger. I ran toward the catacomb, hitting two rungs at a time, waving the group toward the tunnel.

The girls and the boy picked up Fleming, chair and all, bringing him in. Noah followed. I fumbled for an altar candle, lit it, and continued on.

Down in the lower chamber I helped Fleming sit down. Mitzy, holding her machine gun, and Tara slumped against the wall. The boy huddled close to Noah.

The rock around us quaked and a dull explosion echoed off the tunnel walls. Another came before the sound faded, then others. A stick of bombs plastered the grounds above us. Dust and acrid gases filtered through, stinging our nostrils. There were five drops in quick succession.

Claustrophobia took hold of Tara. She scampered up the steps. I went after her, caught her at the top and held her tightly. There was silence. No more explosions shook the headland. The first wave of planes had gone. Now we could expect choppers and more parachutists sent to see what the bombs had accomplished. I needed to be on top to meet them.

I started up and discovered I wasn't alone. Everybody had enough of that graveyard. Tara, Mitzy and the boy were at my heels; Fleming and a groggy Noah, supporting each other, followed.

THIRTEEN

The altar was covered with a layer of stone fragments, and there was a fresh hole over it in the ceiling. Maybe one of the old man's gods felt left out of his big-wind dance. The room above was intact—the entrance open and only the stone-slab door blown off. The parade was pocked with gaping pits, and the rubble spread from wall to wall. The turret above the breakwater had taken a direct hit—it simply wasn't there any more. A few of the rooms were gone, and the fortress wall behind one of them was leveled.

The old patriarch dropped a hand onto Fleming's shoulder, surveying the damage. His jaw was set in deep anger. He turned to look out across the mountain top, thought for a minute, then said something in patois to the doctor. Whatever he said brought a half-certain, half-speculative smile from the president of Grand LaClare Island.

Over the treetops a huge blue-black cloud was moving toward us. The trees were thrashing, their pale leaves shimmering. Through the new hole in the wall I could see the waves rising. As I stood watching the cove entrance, I spotted a long gray shape nosing gingerly through—a Corvette. I wondered what she thought her light guns could accomplish that the bomb sticks hadn't already done.

Beside me Mitzy Gardner chuckled. "Beautiful little beast, isn't she. What do you think Jerome's navy will try now?"

"I don't think this ship is his. She's flying a Cuban flag, but I'll lay odds that her skipper's name is something like Ivan, not Juan. She's an antisubmarine ship—carries eggs in her belly. She may think she can mine the cliff and blow us up."

If so, she would have to lay in close or use frogmen, and I could handle them. The rest of our party came to watch her approach. She was barely moving, feeling her way through the shallows, heading toward the breakwater. I didn't think she'd come in far enough to hit it, but I couldn't help hoping she would.

She didn't. She hove to just beyond the reach of our guns and put four black-suited swimmers over the side, lowering depth charges to them. They submerged. I gave them time to come well within range, then sprayed a pattern of lead in the water, working out from the base across their probable path. The first passes didn't get results. But the next one did.

The water erupted in a boiling spout. The swimmers were bunched. All four charges went off together. Tons of water and scraps of black flew into the air. Water rushed in on the enormous spout, and when it subsided, a wave rose, circling outward. the force of concussion in the shallow water drove the wave hard into the Corvette, hitting her broadside and slamming her hard over. She took sea on the low side, wallowing back as the wave crashed over her and stayed aboard. It was too much weight. She lay sloshing, rolling sluggishly in the growing swells.

I didn't think she would float long. The black cloud was billowing upward. The wind roared, and whitecaps ran before it.

At first I didn't hear the other sound. But suddenly a squadron of chopper gun ships came into view. It was lousy flying weather for the helicopters, but lives are the cheapest commodity the communist countries have.

"Take cover." I had to shout against the noise. "They'll attack us here, then set one down. Get moving!"

Noah and the boy lifted Fleming and carried him toward the tunnel, with Tara Sawyer behind them. Mitzy and I brought up the rear. Tara got as far as the stairs, then swung back, defiant.

"Damn it, I'm tired of being useless. Show me how to use one of these guns and let me play too."

The girl had guts, and I was proud of her. I gave her a quick lesson, emphasizing that she had to be sure where she was aiming before she touched the trigger.

"You stay here, Tara," I told her. "Mitzy, pick another hole. I'll take the other side. Let the bird land and try for the men after they're outside. We may take a ride after all."

I watched Mitzy run for a room farther down the row. Then I dashed across the corner of the parade as the flap of props came closer and closer. I was hardly under the roof when the choppers went over, tattooing the walls and floor with fifty caliber slugs. After they passed over, I stepped out and fired at the

underside of the nearest one. It went out of control
and wobbled out of sight toward the jungle. I heard
Mitzy Gardner's gun chatter. She scored a partial hit
but didn't cripple the bird. Tara caught on too late
and wasted half a clip on the retreating choppers.

With all the noise their cannons were making, they
didn't even realize they were being fired on. They
came back to hover over us, covering the landing of
the ship I'd disabled.

A slash of heavy rain drummed across the parade.

The chopper settled to the ground, touching down
like a weary bird. The door opened on the side opposite me, and a machine gun sprayed the walls that
hid the girls. Then the pilot climbed out and ran
around the nose of the ship while a gun inside kept
him covered. I heard both girls' guns track the pilot.
He sprawled on his face in a pool of blood. The man
in the chopper was still shooting in our direction.
From where I stood, I couldn't see him, so I ducked
out of the room and dashed toward the chopper to
get a look at him. I had to stop that gun. I fired
through the glass and saw the gunner's head dissolve
into red pulp.

The rain was coming down in sheets now. The sky
was an ugly greenish black. Lightning flashed, and
thunder deafened me. The chopper bounced in the
gale winds. The other copters couldn't fight the
storm. They turned back to try to set down on the
beach. I was running to get some rope to tie down
the captured bird when Mitzy's shrill scream stopped
me. She was pointing dumbly into the room where
Tara had been.

I knew what had happened before I got there. Tara Sawyer lay there, her beautiful body torn to shreds and awash with blood. One short look and I got out of there fast. I couldn't stop to think. There was a plane to anchor. But I was clumsy at the job. My mind wasn't on it. Poor Tara! She shouldn't have chosen to fight.

Mitzy was with me, knotting lines from the chopper around big uprooted rocks. I tied one around her waist to keep her from being blown away. By the time the plane was anchored, we had to crawl back to shelter an inch at a time, hanging on to stones. The wind had to be over a hundred miles an hour.

We didn't go to the tunnel. I didn't want to see Tara again right away. And I had some thinking to do. I didn't want to face Noah, either. He had asked for a hurricane, he got it. In February, no less. I wondered how.

We sat without talking, each of us filled with our own unhappy thoughts. The storm lasted an hour before it let up. There was an ominous calm. In the Southern Hemisphere hurricanes blow clockwise; in the North they blow counter-clockwise, wheeling as they move. The velocity increases from the center toward the outer edge. Unless Noah had a curve on this one, we would soon be taking a real battering from the opposite direction.

But there was still time to see what damage the first half had accomplished. The downpour had stopped, and the parade steamed. Through the hole in the wall we saw the Corvette. It was hard aground, breaking up. The choppers were roosting in trees, and the stranded patrol boat was gone. The smashed yachts and tugs had been flung ashore. The sky was empty.

FOURTEEN

I turned back from surveying the cove and found Noah walking curiously around the chopper, nodding to himself. But when he came toward us, his face was drawn, his eyes troubled.

I said in a voice as even as I could keep it, "You did yourself proud, and I confess I can't explain it. You even brought us a taxi to take the doctor off."

His lips twitched briefly, but he remained somber. "Miss Sawyer. She is a loss to us all. One art I am not capable of is resurrection. But we can give her an honored place among our heros."

A voodoo burial for Tara? I didn't think so. Her father wouldn't appreciate that. I planned to take her body with us, but I decided not to discuss it then. Noah was still talking.

"The wind will come again soon. These structures," he flapped a hand toward the quadrangle of rooms, "have been jarred by the bombs, weakened. When the storm returns, the walls will crumble. It would be best if you joined us below."

He didn't wait for us to agree but started toward the tunnel, then disappeared. Mitzy and I followed. I stopped for a minute over Tara. It made me sick and angry. It would be a pleasure to use every AXE technique I knew on Colonel Carib Jerome.

169

There were now two short candles burning on the altar, one of thanks, I supposed, and one of supplication. We were going to need all the help we could get. Noah was busy with prayer sticks, maybe clearing Tara's way to wherever he expected her to go.

I wasn't needed there. I felt caged and restless. I wasn't even aware that I was pacing back and forth till Noah turned and said softly, "You need not remain just here, Mr. Carter. This is a labyrinth; there are other rooms you might care to explore." He touched a stone that looked like part of the wall, and it swung inward, onto a passage.

His words held a hint of accusation—I was obviously disrupting his ceremonies, and I was glad enough to leave. I still had candles in my pocket, and I lighted one. Then Mitzy and I stepped through the hidden door, and Noah closed it behind us. Steps twisted downward; the corridor branched off into paths cut out of soft limestone.

We found a room with a wide well in the middle. This was where water was caught and stored for times of siege. Other rooms served as root cellars— they were cold enough to keep food for long periods of time. Still another was a "butcher shop," filled with hanging carcasses. I had wondered how the old man had fed his hungry horde when they couldn't safely hunt outside the walls.

For an hour we wandered from one dead end to another, yet there was always enough fresh air. I wanted to find the source. Following the angle to the candle flame, we walked along a curving passage that spiralled up toward the surface. Just when I thought

we were almost at ground level, we came to a pad-
locked iron grille that blocked the passage. I worked
at the lock with my stiletto, and it finally fell open.
We moved on past the grille and up a flight of steps
to the second corner turret. Air was coming in
through the open gun slots.

The outer door of the turret was barred on the inside. I lifted the bar, and we continued on up a maha-
gony stairway up to a trap door that opened into the
upper turret room. Mitzy had said it in the begin-
ning—nobody had seen all the old faker's surprises.

This was obviously a radio room. It was filled with
sending and receiving equipment—the best.

I sat in front of the console on a bamboo chair and
suddenly began to laugh. Mitzy reacted differently.
She was furious.

"Why, that damned old hypocritical con man!"
she yelled. "He's given everybody the shaft. He shoos
us out of his fake *houmfort* so he can make his chick-
en magic in private. Then he patters up here to pick
up a weather report. No wonder he was so damned
certain there'd be a hurricane."

"And he rubbed our noses in it with that wild act,"
I added. "He had me talking to myself. Jungle
drums! I bet you'll find another outfit hidden in the
bushes, broadcasting up to the second news on the
Port of Spain front. Let's find out what's happening
in the world."

I flipped a few switches, and a lightbulb glowed
overhead. The power plant hummed as the set came
to life. But the only sound that came through was the
crackle of static. Too much electricity from the

storm to let anything else through. I shut it down.

The gun ports in the radio room were boarded shut. We couldn't see out, but the howl of wind and the roar of torrential rain told us the hurricane was back in full force. Judging by the length of the first half, this storm would blow over before we found our way back to the others.

I locked the grille on our way back. I'd be damned if I was going to let on to Noah that I'd discovered his game. An hour later, when I walked past the wily old man on my way up to check on the chopper, I kept a straight face. But it wasn't easy.

The worst of the storm was over. But the helicopter was gone! At least it wasn't where we had left it. I went out to look around, squinting against the rain that filled my eyes. The chopper lay smashed up against the wall, the long prop blades broken, the engine splintered by a giant tree trunk felled by the wind.

Now the radio was our only link to the outside. But we wouldn't be able to get through for the next couple of hours. The sky grew even blacker with the coming night. Even if I could have gotten through to Hawk, he wouldn't have been able to get a chopper through the storm. So the hell with it till morning.

I had a picture of what the island must look like —just a tangle of trees blocking the roads. Jerome couldn't send any vehicles over them, and he wouldn't try an air attack at night. His boats couldn't make it, either, till the raging sea subsided.

I went down to break the news.

FIFTEEN

We were eating a glum supper of Noah's rations when the unflappable old giant raised his head, listening. I heard it then—the sound of jubilant voices shouting outside. Noah beat me to the stairs by two jumps. He was halfway across the parade when I went through the upper door.

The tribe was back. Noah threw the gate wide, and they streamed in. The tall man translated as the story was told. They had hidden in caves across the island till the hurricane subsided. Then they heard the drums from Port of Spain—the capital was wrecked, the army in disarray. And Jerome was dead!

They were dismayed at the condition of the fortress, but they could make repairs now that they were safe. As they settled in for a night of celebration, Mitzy and I settled in for the night too.

I would have to wait for morning to find proof that my mission was accomplished. I had to see the colonel's body with my own eyes, take fingerprints for AXE. The tribe had heard his body was still in the Sawyer Hotel, so that was where I'd have to go as soon as I could figure a way to get there. If the truck was in working condition, I might be able to drive. I'd take a machete crew along to clear a path.

It would be faster than hiking—if the truck hadn't gone the way of the boats and planes.

Sometime after midnight we finally got to sleep.

In the morning I decided against calling Hawk for help. I don't like to give up on an assignment. Hawk said it was imperative for me to go it alone, and there was still a chance I could put Fleming into office by myself.

The doctor was all for hopping on his white charger and rushing to the rescue of the battered island. But Noah prevailed again. Jungle drums were all well in their way, but he hadn't yet heard any hard news on the radio. Of course, he didn't mention that. He just delegated a group of sturdy young men to clear the road, and we trooped over to the truck.

It looked all right, sitting under an arch of half-toppled trees. I put the rotor in, cleaned the water out of the carburetor, pumped in new gas, and got out from under the hood. Mitzy Gardner was in the front seat, spreading leaves over the soggy upholstery, her machine gun resting on the dashboard.

I didn't argue. She had earned the right to sit in at the finish. The whole tribe pitched in and hauled debris out of the ruts. They cleared the way to the shore road and a mile beyond. We were on our own, with only the crew in the truck to help us. It could have been worse, The trees that blocked the highway were small and easy enough to move. The road had been washed out where it ran close to the sea. But the crew used fallen branches to fill in the depressions. Then I shoved the gear into low as they heaved against the tailgate, and we wallowed on through.

The day was bright, the sky an innocent blue, and the sea calm. But the beaches were like graveyards of little boats, and the pretty ranch houses had been destroyed. Walls were down; roofs lay torn and twisted many yards away; and furniture littered lawns. The first building we passed at close range, the old Poinciana resort, was nothing more than a collapsed heap of timber. Noah's boys dropped off there to root in the wreckage. Beyond it, the native village was a mess—empty-eyed people wandered around, picking up a scrap of something, dropping it, then going to another.

The ancient fort on the hill, which had weathered many other blows over the last couple of hundred years, had survived this one.

Government Plaza was in fairly good shape, but the glass was gone from the windows and the grounds were covered with fallen trees and litter. The soldiers in the area were unarmed and dazed, moving around like zombies in a feeble effort to clean up the grounds. There were other soldiers in the business section, working under junior officers. They glanced at us as we rolled by but made no move to stop us. With their colonel gone, they were in limbo, without authority to send down orders.

At the Sawyer Grand LaClare all the landscaping was uprooted, large trees strewn around like so many twigs. The late afternoon sun glittered red on the piles of splintered glass that surrounded the building. Beyond it, the oily harbor was nearly empty. Only a few small boats floated, hull up, on the long, smooth swells. The water was an ugly, dirty color, heavy with sand. A boom off some wreckage drifted up against the shore, and more rigging fouled the white beach. There were no guards anywhere around.

I pulled up in front of the main entrance, and we got down with our guns. Jerome, I assumed, would be laid out in state in the lobby or casino, with an honor guard watching over him. I would have to get rid of them. But I was wrong. Our feet crunched across the broken glass, and we walked right on in without being stopped.

The lobby was empty, and so was the casino. The entire hotel was a shambles.

"Chip's office maybe?" Mitzy suggested.

We went that way. The black hall attendant was not behind the cashier's desk. To my surprise the electric lock worked, and we went through to the hall. There wasn't a soul in sight. The button controlling Capolla's door opened it. Jerome was not laid out there, either, but the money he had looted was. I heard a deep sigh of relief beside me. When I looked at Mitzy her red tongue was slowly circling her lips.

"The Miami boys will be glad to know this, at least," she said. "I expect Sawyer will reopen."

"But where is Jerome's body?" I wondered aloud. Mitzy thought it might have been taken to Capolla's penthouse.

"You go find out, Nick. I'd better hang around in here. This town is going to begin coming to sometime soon, and I wouldn't want this bundle to disappear now."

"I don't like to leave you alone," I told her. "There could be a mob."

Her lips curled. "The door locks from the inside, and it can't be opened from the hall. This place is a vault. You know how to use the remote control on the elevator?"

I did. I had watched when we first used it. She closed and locked the sliding panel after me, and I hit the button, got into the cage, and tapped the "up" switch. The elevator started to climb. I didn't even feel the car stop. But the door opened silently, and I stepped out onto the deep carpet.

The movement in the little entry hall was too fast for me. I'd barely caught it in my peripheral vision when a hand holding a gun came slashing down at my head. I reacted instinctively and ducked, but the blow caught my neck, paralyzing my arm. My machine gun thudded on the floor, and I couldn't bend my elbow to reach the Luger—couldn't even snap out my stiletto.

I jumped back, clawed with my left hand for the wrist that held the gun, and got a grip on. I stood looking right into Jerome's eyes.

So he wasn't dead. He had a huge bump on his forehead. It must have kept him near the edge a long while, but there was nothing ghostly about his muscle. He was a fine physical specimen. And he could fight as dirty as I could.

While my right hand still hung limp and my left held his arm, he threw a hard fist into my chin and a knee into my crotch. I sagged against him in excruciating pain. But I had to get that gun away from him. Our raised arms came down as I slipped toward the floor. Suddenly he released his grip to let me fall. I went to my knees. He jerked his wrist free, fumbling with his gun to take aim. I buried my mouth in his leg, and clamped my teeth on him, and held on. He screamed and bent double over my back. The gun fell to the floor. I ground my teeth sideways. As he screamed again, I felt hot blood running through his pants. Then my fingers found the gun. I heaved up, dumped him over my shoulders, turned on one knee, and shot him. It spoiled the exquisite agony on his contorted face.

I flexed my right hand for a minute back to its strength. Then I pulled the colonel into the elevator cage. I took his fingerprints, fingers and all, with the stiletto, wrapped them in his handkerchief, and stuffed them in my pocket.

When I got down to the first floor I was surprised to see that Mitzy was still there. When I called her on the intercom, she opened the door.

"Did you find him?"

"I found him."

"Nick, I've been thinking. I can't sit on this nest forever. Let's load up the truck and take the money up to Noah's, where it will be safe."

"All right. Wait here while I bring the truck to the garage."

I got the truck, then moved Jerome out of the way and out of sight. We stowed the money under a tarpaulin and headed back to the hills.

We were almost at the capital fort when a jeep peeled down the drive and blocked the road in front of us. Cuban penants fluttered from the fenders. A colonel in Russian uniform stepped out of the rear, drawing his revolver, and came toward us, shouting.

"All vehicles are ordered off the streets. You had the order . . ." Then he saw Mitzy's red head and gaped. "Who the hell are you? What are you doing in that truck?"

I brought the machine gun up over the dash and shot him. After I disposed of the officer and the driver in the jeep, I drove on up the slope and around the blockage, accelerator floored. So that was why there weren't any senior island army officers in the open—they were in the fort for briefing on their new status, being told what their place was and to stay in it. There wasn't even any pursuit. Nobody was around to see us. Port of Spain was under the martial law of a foreign power.

We were well out of town when we came to the tribe. With Noah at the head, they were marching toward us. Doctor Fleming rode in a litter chair, on the shoulders of as many men as would fit under the shafts. His head was high, his eyes glowing with confidence.

I groaned and stopped. How in hell had he conned the old men into this stunt? With God only knew how many foreign troops in the city! I got down and stood in front of the black giant. I began to shout at him, but he wouldn't even consider turning back. I described the town, the takeover. No reaction.

"With Jerome gone, the people will revolt," he said. "They will support the doctor."

With what? Machetes? Noah stepped around me

and walked serenely on. The tribe flowed around the truck, singing, pounding on drums. I gave up, climbed aboard, and started to turn the truck around. But Mitzy grabbed the wheel.

"You're not taking that load back, lover. This goes up the mountain if I have to take it alone."

Loyalties. Well, she was only on loan to AXE because of Fleming. If the damned fool insisted on getting himself killed, she was going to look out for her Mafia playmates. Okay by me. At least it would keep her out of the massacre. I jumped off with the machine gun and caught up with the head of the column.

The noise behind me grew louder as we went. Looking back, I saw people from the lowlands coming out of the brush, joining the tribe.

The whole native village sprouted like dragon teeth. Rivers of people came down from the hillside houses. The city residents arrived. Then the damnedest thing happened. The native army boiled out of the fort. I figured it was the end, but their backs were toward us, their guns blazing at the building. Then I understood. Jerome's forces had gone along with him till they discovered what he really had in mind—till the Russians told them. Now they were revolting. The common soldiers were for Fleming. The officers who had secretly wanted him were outside with the boys. The men who opted for the Cubans and the handful of Russian "advisers" sent to help Jerome were bottled up in the fort, shooting through the broken door.

The mob surrounded the hill now. A mob knows no

fear. Yelling, knives waving, it moved on in a wave. Many fell under fire. But many more reached the walls, climbed up the vines and through windows to the upper floor. The shooting from the doorway stopped. The guns in there had turned to face the attack within. The native army rushed the entrance. In half an hour the shooting was over. The horde that had gone in through the windows flowed out through the door. There were no Cubans or native officers with them.

The uniformed ranks outside moved into formation and marched down to where Fleming had halted. They saluted and offered their allegiance. President Fleming was home to stay.

SIXTEEN

There wasn't a plane on the airfield that could fly. In the harbor only one fair sized boat floated. The foreign pilots were rounded up, the remnants of the invading people dug out of hiding, all put aboard and sent off.

Under Fleming's efficient, swift command an organized cleanup was begun. Noah's tribe went home. General Hammond's family invited Fleming to occupy the Palace with them until the airfield could be cleared to receive traffic, when they would leave the island. Mitzy sent a runner with a note. Would I ask Davey Hawk to tell Miami where she was and that she'd sit on the nest egg until she had orders.

"Tara Sawyer was given a funeral with all the stops out," she wrote. "She lies on a slab down in the catacombs."

I stayed a week to give Fleming what hand I could and be sure the calm would last. He didn't need my help. It was a vacation. Without a girl to my name.

When I got back to Washington, Sawyer was in the office, raising hell with Hawk about his daughter's death, demanding to bury her at home. I hadn't briefed the old man by phone about Tara. Now Hawk let me handle the problem. I tried to ease Sawyer's pain by building up his daughter's part in saving

Fleming's life, praising her, repeating the full gratitude of the natives. Sawyer gradually quited down,
some of the sorrow turning to pride.

I didn't say anything about Mitzy. Why start a
war between him and the Mafia? Besides, if the girl
could cream something off the top, I thought she had
a right to keep it. Thomas Sawyer could finance the
rebuilding out of profits from his entire chain, and
maybe Mitzy could retire from the Brotherhood.

I told both of them about Noah. Hawk gave me a
fish stare but Sawyer was delighted at the old man's
exploits.

The rest of it I held until after Sawyer left. When
Hawk and I were alone, I set the jar holding Jerome's fingers on the desk. Then with some ceremony
I spread Mitzy Gardner's note in front of my boss.
He glanced at it, then up to meet my eyes. There
wasn't a quiver of muscle, not a tinge of color change
in the parchment face.

"Well." It was his business voice. "I'm waiting for
your report."

I began with the little things. The stewardess; I
was sure Jerome had her murdered, but we'd have to
check it out. The jail Fleming had to fix up. The
dungeons he planned to turn into laboratories for the
university. Then I gave Hawk the rundown on Noah
with a straight face, chronologically.

"He had two hours' warning," I said to Hawk.
"Plenty of time to show how aloof he was from fear
and to put on a one-hour performance. What bothers
me is how the rest of the island got caught so they
didn't get their ships and planes out of danger.

"Could I use your phone?"

He gave permission. I called the weather bureau and got through to a friend there, identified myself and said, "Jim, what time of day did you get the alert on last week's hurricane?"

There was some swearing. "Damn it, Nick, too bloody late to do any good. The satellite didn't pick it up until it was over Grand La Clare lashing its tail. By the time we got a warning out, it was half over. I never knew anything to come up that fast. Even Noah didn't call us."

Something cold started working up my spine. "Do you know about Noah?"

"He's our spotter there. N.O.A.H., his call letters. He's good. Usually picks weather out of the air as fast as we do. Why? You sound funny."

"Uh-uh. Thanks."

I hung up. Hawk hung up the extension.

Hawk sounded hollow. "If he'd reported in, a lot of damage could have been prevented. A lot of lives saved."

"And an island lost to 'big brother'."

I went out of the office softly, closed the door softly. The weather satellite takes constant pictures on one huge hunk of ocean at a time. It didn't see that freak storm until it walloped ashore.

I lit a cigarette and tried to kiss the whole thing off. Threw the cigarette away. The hell with it.

The End

Dear Reader:

We want to thank you for buying this AWARD paperback book, and we do hope that you enjoyed it.

Our aim is to publish books that you want to read. Therefore, we would like to ask a few questions concerning your personal reading habits and preferences.

If you will check off your answers to the questions listed below and return to Award Books, Dept. RJA, 235 E. 45th Street, New York, New York 10017, we will be happy to send you a complimentary copy of one of Award's current releases as our way of saying, "Thank you."

1. I decided to read this book because of:
   ____Personal recommendation
   ____Advertising. Where?
   ____TV ____Radio ____Newspaper ____Magazine
   ____Book cover
   ____Knew of hardcover edition
   ____Other

2. Where did you purchase this book?
   ____Book Store   ____Rail or Bus Terminal
   ____Newsstand   ____Discount Store
   ____Airport   ____Department Store
   ____Supermarket   ____Other

3. My favorite categories are:
   ____Mysteries   ____Police-Action
   ____Westerns   ____Movie Tie-ins
   ____Science Fiction   ____Health and Fitness
   ____Mystic and Occult   ____Cook Books
   ____Antiques   ____Diet

4. I read on the average (paperback):
   ____Under 3 books a year
   ____3 to 6 books a year
   ____6 to 12 books a year
   ____Over 12

5. My age is:
   ____Under 18   ____35 to 49
   ____18 to 24   ____50 to 64
   ____25 to 34   ____65 and over

6. My education (check highest):
   ____High School   ____College Graduate
   ____Attended College   ____Post-Graduate School

Please send my free Award Book to:

Name_____

Address_____

City_____State_____Zip_____

AWARD BOOKS

NICK CARTER

Don't Miss A Single High-Tension Novel In The Nick Carter Killmaster Series

THE Z DOCUMENT

Nick Carter

Nick races to stop an incredible bid for blood-drenched power and wealth deep inside Ethiopia. AQ1460—$1.25

AZTEC AVENGER

Nick Carter

The secret key to an endless supply of free heroin—for sale to the highest bidder on the black market! AQ1356—$1.25

NIGHT OF THE AVENGER

Nick Carter

Killmaster battles a chilling stratagem to build a private empire on the smoldering ruins of the world. AQ1331—$1.25

CODE NAME WEREWOLF

Nick Carter

Carter matches wits and nerves with a ruthless Spanish assassin. AQ1329—$1.25

BEIRUT INCIDENT

Nick Carter

N3 must eliminate the number one Don in the United States—and destroy the Syndicate's new army of killers.

AQ1333—$1.25

THE FILTHY FIVE

Nick Carter

The Chinese back a plot to assassinate the U.S. President.

AQ1415—$1.25

TEMPLE OF FEAR

Nick Carter

World security hangs in the balance as Killmaster fights KGB killers in the orient. AQ1440—$1.25

THE BLACK DEATH

Nick Carter

Voodoo zombies guard a secret missile complex in Haiti, and the countdown for launching has already started!

AQ1401—$1.25

HOUR OF THE WOLF

Nick Carter

Nick Carter gambles against desperate odds to save a deadly nuclear secret from falling into enemy hands. AQ1387—$1.25

THE DEATH'S-HEAD CONSPIRACY

Nick Carter

America's largest cities are doomed to nuclear destruction unless N3 can disarm the elusive human fuse. AN1178—95¢

USE HANDY, MONEY-SAVING ORDER FORM ON BACK PAGE

THE KATMANDU CONTRACT   **Nick Carter**
A kidnap plot by Chinese terrorists leads Killmaster to the Hima-
layas for a rescue attempt more dazzling than the breathtaking
scenery.   AQ1479—$1.25

ICE TRAP TERROR   **Nick Carter**
Killmaster battles an incredible plot to launch a 20th-century
Ice Age!   AN1227—95¢

THE PEKING DOSSIER   **Nick Carter**
An endless wave of programmed assassins is eliminating top
American officials. Nick's assignment—find the mysterious
Chinese mastermind.   AQ1388—$1.25

SIGN OF THE COBRA   **Nick Carter**
The back alleys of India explode with violence as Nick Carter
collides with the invincible might of SHIVA!   AN1270—95¢

TIME CLOCK OF DEATH   **Nick Carter**
The U.S. and Russia in a nuclear showdown. Killmaster races to
stop the inevitable slaughter.   AQ1370—$1.25

STRIKE FORCE TERROR   **Nick Carter**
Nick Carter infiltrates Russia's most notorious slave labor camp
to thwart an electrifying kidnap attempt.   AQ1298—$1.25

SEVEN AGAINST GREECE   **Nick Carter**
Seven powerful men form an alliance of hate against the free
world.   AQ1393—$1.25

SIX BLOODY SUMMER DAYS   **Nick Carter**
A billion-dollar blackmail plot is backed by deadly nuclear artil-
lery. Millions will die if Killmaster doesn't get to the extortionists
in time!   AQ1449—$1.25

14 SECONDS TO HELL   **Nick Carter**
World destruction is just seconds away as Carter battles his way
deep inside Red China.   AQ1448—$1.25

THE ULTIMATE CODE   **Nick Carter**
N3 on the trail of a vital decoding machine—and in the middle
of an international espionage coup that threatens world disaster!
AQ1486—$1.25

USE HANDY, MONEY-SAVING ORDER FORM ON BACK PAGE

"NICK CARTER OUT-BONDS JAMES BOND!"
—BUFFALO NEWS

AGENT COUNTER-AGENT
Nick Carter
A bizarre threat to American sovereignty catapults Nick into a mind-bending game of wits and nerves with the notorious KGB.
AQ1477—$1.25

ASSASSINATION BRIGADE
Nick Carter
Killmaster faces an army of kamikaze slaves and a mad super-genius bent on world conquest!
AQ1456—$1.25

ASSASSIN: CODE NAME VULTURE
Nick Carter
Killmaster must stop the bloody coup-masters led by the international assassin named Vulture!
AQ1454—$1.25

MASSACRE IN MILAN
Nick Carter
Arab terrorists, Nazi spies and Israeli counter-agents—colliding in a deadly game of oil diplomacy and espionage.
AQ1455—$1.25

RUSH YOUR ORDER TODAY!